MOTHERHOOD MADE

A MAN OUT OF ME

MOTHERHOOD MADE
A MAN OUT OF ME

KAREN KARBO

BLOOMSBURY

Published by Bloomsbury USA, New York and London.
Distributed to the trade by St. Martin's Press.

Library of Congress Cataloging-in-Publication Data has been applied for

ISBN 1–58234–154–0

First published in the US by
Bloomsbury Publishing in 2000

This paperback edition published 2001

10 9 8 7 6 5 4 3 2 1

Typeset by Hewer Text Ltd, Edinburgh
Printed in the United States of America
by R.R. Donnelley & Sons company, Harrisonburg, Virginia

For Fiona

1

I am a terrible mother. I love my daughter, love her so much
I'm amazed I actually have to hold her in my arms, that she
doesn't just stick to my side, my heart heavy as a black hole,
dense with love, trying to suck her into it. I love her like this,
then, minutes later, can't wait to get out of the house, leaving
her behind. I'm told all mothers are like this, more or less, and
are all racked with guilt because of it.

The week I found out about Mary Rose, my beloved Stella
Marie was six months old. She had black stick-straight-up
hair, blueberry eyes that would find their way eventually to a
less exotic shade of hazel, an abiding affection for the decorative moldings of our seventy-year-old house.

She liked to gaze at the corners of windows and doors, reach
out as if to grab them, then wag her hands excitedly, like a
palsied lady trying to open a wide-mouth jar. Her basic look
was one of consternation. She was not a silly baby, even
though I'd been known to make her wear a bonnet. She is
perfect. The world's cutest human. *Really* the world's cutest
human.

And yet, one needs a break. All I wanted to do was go to the
grocery store.

'I love Stella, I'm just not interested in changing her
diapers,' said Lyle, when I asked if he might watch her for

an hour. Made me feel as if I was asking for the keys to the car and ten bucks for gas.

'*Interested* in? We're not talking a PBS documentary on marsupials here, Lyle. She's your daughter.'

'Here's something I read that's kind of cool – did you know that newborn kangaroos find their way into the pouch completely unassisted by their mothers?'

'Don't do the changing-the-subject thing. Please?' I rolled the portable dishwasher as close to Stella's bedroom doorway as I could without disconnecting the nozzle from the kitchen sink. The Perfect Wonderment had been up seven times during the night, but still wasn't sleepy. The dishwasher was my secret weapon. The *whir-whoosh whir-whoosh* of the water sloshing around was better than any lullaby. I could hear Stella in her crib, doing one of her Stella monologues in which she seemed to fall back on a word that sounded a lot like *intaglio*.

'Are there even any dishes in there?' said Lyle. He stood in the kitchen frowning at the dishwasher, as if it were one of his computer problems, his collie eyes made slightly larger by his glasses. He'd lost weight since Stella came, mostly because dinner now was us standing in the middle of the kitchen, eating whatever straight from the refrigerator: cheese, peanut butter on celery, Nestlé chocolate-chip cookie dough straight from its yellow tube.

'If you don't want to help, don't criticize.'

'I'm not criticizing, I'm just saying. It's a waste of water.'

'If Stella sleeps, and I get to take a nap some time before the new year, then it's not a goddamned waste of water.'

'I thought we agreed we were going to lay off the profanity. You know, in front of Stella. And I do want to help. I *said* I wanted to help.'

'As long as it's something convenient, you're all for helping. If it's a gorgeous day and Stella needs a little air, you'll walk her around the block. That's your definition of helping. It's like when you're playing on the computer and you tell someone you have to get off and go baby-sit. Baby-sitting is what you do for kids that aren't your own. It's what you do when you're fifteen and want a chance to make a few bucks and see what there is to eat in someone else's kitchen. You don't baby-sit your own daughter.'

'Well . . .' He pinched the end of his nose, something he always did when he wondered if he should say what he was thinking. '. . . guys do.'

'You know what it's like, what you do? And probably all men for that matter. It's like the difference between a deaf person signing as a means of communication and a lovely, well-intentioned hearing person signing as a show of solidarity.'

'You're starting to go off, Brooke.'

'I am not going off. Why do you say I'm going off whenever I'm trying to make a point.'

'Why don't you just go get the turkey?'

'Why don't *you* just go get the turkey.'

'I thought that's what this was all about. You wanted to get out of the house and you wanted me to baby-sit Stella, and I asked – just asked, so sue me – when you'd last changed her diaper.'

'So you could be sure you wouldn't have to change one. Look, you think I enjoy changing diapers?'

'Yeah, I do.'

Okay, he was right. I did tend to rhapsodize about the wonder of Stella's 'projects.' Steam and cut a carrot into bite-sized bits and a mere twelve hours later there they are again, bright and square as ever, cradled in her diaper amid an aromatic little dollop of guacamole-ish doo. I don't expect the mailman to find this amazing, but I'd like to think that Stella's own father would take an interest. Is that asking too much? I already know the answer.

3

The dishwasher did the trick, as I knew it would, and I went out to buy the turkey. Donleavy's Market is beloved by every impractical person in a ten-square-mile radius. It sells huge, pale bars of French soap and bottles of olive oil for every occasion. (Lyle and I used to like to joke that 'Extra Extra Virgin' should be repunctuated to reflect modern sexual reality – Extra Extra: Virgin!)

When I pulled into the driveway behind the market, I saw the lavender Mowers and Rakers truck parked near the back fence. It was hard to miss. It's a civic institution. The sides were smartly painted with a Gauguin-inspired profusion of red passion flowers, pink hollyhocks, marigolds, iris, and cosmos, green vines creeping up the M of Mowers, the R of Rakers.

A few yards to the right of the truck, Mary Rose stood on the top rung of a twelve-foot ladder, pruning a fig tree that grew on the adjacent property. Her back was to me, her blond hair held up in a bun with a green pencil. She wore baggy plaid shorts and a gray sweatshirt with the sleeves cut off, even though it was forty degrees and raining. Mary Rose was six feet tall and lanky, with broad shoulders and large feet. She was my age, thirty-five, and was a teenager at a time when any woman over five-eight had a cruel nickname, always a variation on the theme of Amazon. As a result, Mary Rose slouched. She sang along with her Walkman, her pruners flashing around among the big, wet leaves, swaying along with the music. This was so Mary Rose. Not simply standing on the top rung of a ladder, but further pressing her luck by rocking back and forth.

To say Mary Rose was a gardener would be selling her short. Yard maintenance in our city was no luxury. In the spring, blackberry shoots grew eight inches a day and the conscientious mowed their lawns every seventy-two hours. Failure to routinely clip, prune, thin, and weed meant a yard reclaimed by forest, a house under attack by wild clematis and morning glory. In our city, it really was a jungle out there.

I admired Mary Rose, and Mary Rose's life. She was smart, resolute. She kept her own hours and got to work outside. I kept my own hours, too, but as a producer, I spent most of them trying to talk people into things they didn't want to do. I had to deal with Hollywood people, which had to be much worse than coping with housewives worried about the health of their delphiniums.

This is what I was thinking as I went into Donleavy's: how Mary Rose was a modern-day . . . who was the goddess whose named started with an *A*, the one who was independent and sporty and said what she thought? I didn't bother with a shopping cart, I could carry what I needed.

Mary Rose wasn't like any other woman I knew. She never perched on the edge of the sofa with a pint of Ben & Jerry's, wondering why she didn't have a man, or if she was seeing someone why, in the end, he would prove to be wrong for her. She didn't worry that she spent too much time working, or not enough time working. She didn't fret about whether she should have an eye tuck, then worry that she was superficial for worrying about whether she should have an eye tuck. Was it Aphrodite?

I took a turkey from the display in the small meat department. A life-size scarecrow cutely pointed at the stack of birds. They were free-range or had never been frozen, or both. I didn't bother with the beautifully calligraphed fine print. I picked one up, cradled it in the crook of my arm. Eleven pounds eight ounces, about like Stella.

Aramaic? No, that was a dead language. Or an aftershave. Lyle would know the name of the goddess, except I was irritated with Lyle, was always irritated with Lyle these days, and would punish him by not asking him when I got home. What about cranberry sauce? Did Lyle like the kind with the berries or without? The kind that retains an imprint of the inside of the can when you slide it onto the dish, or not? Aramis? No that *was* the aftershave. Maybe I'd just skip the cranberry sauce altogether. Lyle didn't care about Thanksgiving one way or the other, so why was I even bothering? Lyle thought we should take advantage of the fact that Stella was still clueless, as he liked to put it, and go to our favorite Tex-Mex restaurant on Thanksgiving, where there was usually an hour and a half wait but would be empty on the holiday.

Outside, it was drizzling. I started to run, so Stella wouldn't get wet, then heard someone behind me yelling. 'Miss, oh Miss!' I turned to see a police officer – blond brush-cut, forearms the size of my thighs – trotting up behind me. His gold nameplate said Beckett. 'You haven't paid for that.'

'Paid for . . . oh, *oh*! I thought . . .' I looked down, expecting to see Stella in her little red fleece jacket and cap, but there was the turkey in my arms instead. The fleshy, nonfrozen breast stared blankly up at me. It seems I was also patting it in a reassuring manner. 'I thought this was my baby! I mean, I mistook her . . . it . . .' I started to snort. Lyle calls it my grandmother laugh. 'This is only the second time I've been out of the house without Stella, so naturally, it was just *habit* . . . Stella is much prettier than . . .' I couldn't stop laughing.

Beckett said he also had a six-month-old. We swapped war stories. He said his wife had inadvertently given him a black eye during a particularly hairy patch of labor.

I said, 'Hate to break the news, but it wasn't inadvertent. I'm sorry. I didn't mean that. I'm sure your wife appreciates you very much. I'm sure you're one of those guys who makes "involved father" sound like God's truth instead of an oxymoron.'

Beckett gave a hardy PR laugh, the kind that displayed his

molars to their best advantage, but he didn't take his eyes off me.

'Oh! The turkey. Let me just get my wallet. Do I pay you – or no, I just probably go get back in line . . .' I pawed around inside my shoulderbag. No wallet. 'Let me just . . .' I moved the turkey to the crook of my left arm, so I could check my jeans pockets and the pockets of my coat. I have an informal banking system where I leave five-dollar bills in rarely visited pockets, for moments just like this. Two nickels and a penny. This was not good. This was starting to look like shoplifting. 'I must have left my wallet at home.'

Beckett took the turkey from me and stuck it under his arm. You could tell he used to play football. A few shoppers in the parking lot dawdled over unlocking their cars, allowing them to stare. Beckett clapped me on the shoulder. 'I'll let it go this time with a recommendation: Get more sleep.'

I had the presence of mind not to blurt out 'Easy for you to say!' which is, I suppose, a testimony to my fundamental sanity. I kept quiet, felt my face get hot, then, as I watched him turn around and go back into Donleavy's, thought I might cry. Tired, that's all. Tired, and now turkeyless.

At that moment Mary Rose came over. 'What was that all about?' She was pulling a waterproof anorak over her head. Around her waist she wore a tan leather holster, where she kept all her clippers and such. I told her what happened. She lit a cigarette, listened, blew smoke sideways out of her mouth. 'Shake it off. I'm sure the cop sees stuff like this all the time. It's no big deal. Where is Stella, anyway?'

'Home with her father. He can't get enough of her, you know? I practically have to wrestle him to the ground to get her away from him, just so I can feed her. Joined at the hip. Fathers and daughters, you know how they are. From birth they're that way. Joined at the hip. Wait, did I already say that?'

I heard my voice go wobbly. Is this what motherhood had reduced me to? Weeping in the parking lot of Donleavy's, wiping my nose with the cuff of my sweater? I tried to remember who I was: a producer of independent films, a baker of berry pies, an occasional runner, the world's only adult lover of the knock-knock joke. A sometimes skier. A collector of funny ashtrays. The wife of Lyle. The mother of Stella. Brooke Stellamom.

Mary Rose considered me from beneath her bangs. Artemis. That's the goddess I was thinking of. The virgin goddess of the hunt. The no-time-for-nonsense goddess.

Mary Rose was not one of those women who believed housekeeping extended to tidying up conversations, filling in all the awkward moments with decorative remarks. 'You and Lyle should come with me to the Barons' for Thanksgiving. I don't think Ward would mind my asking you.'

I said it sounded like fun! I said I'd ask Lyle and give her a call tomorrow. I hopped in the Volvo (pumpkin-colored, formerly owned by someone with a thing for incontinent cats and vanilla-scented air fresheners), buckled up, gave a goofy wave, and sped off, the Volvo fish-tailing as I hit a patch of soggy maple leaves. I have a peculiar habit. The more bizarre a situation is, the more I'm compelled to pretend it's as normal as can be.

Mary Rose and the Barons? Audra and Big Hank Baron were among Mary Rose's biggest clients. I was also related to them in some convoluted fashion which, I'm embarrassed to say, I never remember accurately. I think my grandfather, who had a stroke at the age of fifty-six and didn't speak for the next twenty years, is Audra Baron's uncle. Before the stroke, my mother had also been unsure exactly how the Barons were related to us, and after the stroke she was too shy to ask Poppo to scrawl, on his little blackboard, the answer to the question: *how are we related to the woman with the hair who threw herself on your chest and wept? I forgot.*

The Barons owned one of those West Hills mansions whose grounds boasted trees that were here when Lewis and Clark arrived. They had a foundation (the family, not the house, although obviously the house did too). They had hospital wings named after them. Why would Mary Rose be having Thanksgiving there? *I don't think Ward would mind my asking you . . .* What was *that* about? Audra and Hank's son, Ward, was one of those good-looking men – shoulders, jaw, a serious nose that takes your breath away – whose best qualities are visible at one hundred paces. Women see him, meet him, and know this instantly. But they are waylaid by his giddy jokes ('What's the last thing that goes through a bug's mind before he hits the windshield? His butt!'), thinking, hoping, that a third-grade sense of humor is an indicator of wit and character.

I decided that Audra and Big Hank were probably out of town, and Ward was having one of his parties. I remember having heard that he was living at home while his houseboat, moored ten miles west of our city in an anchorage full of artists, filmmakers, and nuts with money, was being refurbished.

It turned out to be nothing like that at all.

The Barons lived high in the West Hills on a ridge of rudely verdant forest. The house itself was a local curiosity; built in the 1920s with money pilfered from the government by the owner of our region's largest shipyard, it was a three-story Mediterranean villa with raked concrete walls and a terracotta tile roof. From the front windows there was a view of three mountains, two rivers, and our lovely downtown.

The only other time I'd had Thanksgiving at the Barons' was during the filming of my first movie, *Romeo's Dagger*, ten years earlier, when Audra was infused with the extravagant feelings of connectedness that always go with making a movie, then dissipate the morning after the wrap party quicker than a

throat full of helium sucked from a balloon. Since then, I had
seen very little of them, although I occasionally ran into Audra
around town.

When Mary Rose and I arrived a little after 4:00 on
Thanksgiving Day, Audra gave Mary Rose, Stella, and me a
big flapping-hand welcome, kissing the air beside our ears.
'Brooke, it's been too long. And there's that adorable baby.
Are you sure Lyle doesn't have any Asian in him anywhere?
Little Stella looks as exotic as a little Tatar. Maybe it's just that
black hair. From what I remember of your mother's side of the
family they're *dishwater.*' She swooped down on Stella and
left an orange lipstick butterfly on her temple. Stella gave her
that furrow-browed baby stare, the same one you see everyday on displeased senators on CNN. I thought I would pop
with pride. No one has more dignity than a six-month-old.

Audra was impressively slim, with thick, highly managed
auburn hair. She was one of a vanishing breed, a Lady of the
House, who has never held a paying job but has worked
herself silly putting food on the table every night for a passel of
ingrates. Most people look at this kind of old-fashioned
American woman with scorn; they should try getting a meal
for five on the table every night for forty years. Audra was in
her sixties now, and seemed even more frantic than I remembered. Frantic to do things right. Frantic to amuse.
Frantic, of course, to look young. I don't think she understood
that unless you could make yourself look twenty-four, the
Herculean regimen and hocus-pocus involved in looking a
mere ten years younger wasn't worth giving up the pleasures
of tanning and the occasional Twinkie. Or maybe she did
understand. She had a waist, which she liked to emphasize by
wearing wide, colorful belts.

'Where is the Sensitive Photocopier Repairman anyway?'
Audra made her blue eyes twinkle. I felt my jaw clench.

The Sensitive Photocopier Repairman was Lyle. Or what I

used to call Lyle behind his back, when my love for him felt as sturdy as one of the bottom members of a human pyramid. It was cute then, cute and teasingly half accurate. Drunken tiffs, flirtations bordering on infidelity, my backing his new truck into a phone pole, anything was a match for our love. We'd met just after Audra brought me the rights to the story that eventually became *Romeo's Dagger*. My life was insane with possibility. My first feature and true love, all in the same month. That my new man was fastidious to the point of pathology mattered not. It was adorable. Then, as now, every morning he went to work in a bright white button-down broadcloth dress shirt and returned home after a day of messing around the insides of copiers with nary a smudge of toner or streak of grease anywhere on him. How the sensitive part got in there, I couldn't remember. But I didn't like Audra using it now; it wasn't her joke to make.

'Lyle had to host a plague,' I said. 'He's one of the game-masters on an on-line computer game and tonight they're having a plague. The idea was to keep people off the game over the holiday, so they thought if they had an epidemic, people would spend time with their families instead of sub-jecting their characters to festering pustules and dementia. But the gamemasters still have to work.'

'Well, I hope he feels better,' said Audra.

I cut a glance at Mary Rose, who looked uncharacteristically meek. I had never seen her in a dress; this one was burgundy rayon that had 'special occasion' written all over it. She tucked her hair behind her ears with the tips of her fingers over and over. What she does when she's ready to tackle a big problem, like pulling out a hedge. This was not like her. This was not like her at all.

Somewhere around on the other side of the house, male voices could be heard, and a slapping sound, like someone beating out a wet carpet hung on the line.

'That *game!*' said Audra. 'A Baron tradition. Every year the kids drink too much of their father's single malt and play basketball in the rain.'

The kids were Little Hank, age forty-two, Ward, thirty-nine, and Dicky, thirty-three. My cousins. I think.

If Mary Rose and I were other women, or still ourselves at a different time in our lives, we would have been out there with them: playing, pretending to play as a way of aligning ourselves with the good-times-having men (instead of the marshmallow yams-baking women), or standing under the eaves sipping imported beer. But I was happy to sit and hold Stella on my lap, and Mary Rose wanted to talk. We allowed Audra to park us in the study while she hustled back to the kitchen. The study was a grand, clammy room where the green marble fireplace gave off charm but no heat, and the heavy green velvet swag curtains hung like dried seaweed from their gold rods. The woodsy smell of the fire couldn't compete with lonely odor of dampness. It didn't seem as if anyone else was home. There was certainly no party.

'Brooke,' spluttered Mary Rose. 'I have something to tell you. Ward and I. We're . . . *ack!* . . . I don't want to jinx it.' She put her big hands to her face.

'You're what. Not . . . that?'

'Not what?' said Mary Rose.

'There's only one *what* that's *that*,' I said. I felt suddenly as if I was channeling Dr. Seuss.

'Yes,' she said.

'No!' I said.

I couldn't believe it. I couldn't wait to tell Lyle. Lyle once said Mary Rose was the last living Valkyrie. I enthusiastically agreed, then went and looked up *Valkyrie* in the dictionary. Mary Rose, with her own business, vacation time-share, financial portfolio. She even had a .25 Colt automatic slung in a tiny hammock behind her nightstand, which she'd learned to shoot for self-protection.

Mary Rose was too level-headed to fall for Ward. But this is how it is, isn't it? Simpering fools conquer men and nations, strong-headed women in seven-league boots, unused to being the love object, swoon and are lost.

Then I heard about it all. How they met (she was transplanting some perennials; he was bored and trying to find someone to play croquet with him). How Ward liked to chase Mary Rose around the fringes of the Baron property, tackling her and biting the insides of her elbows, the backs of her knees. How Ward composed love poems about Mary Rose's mastery of the sickly rhododendrons by the driveway that no one had ever coaxed into bloom.

The fire flickered exhaustedly in the green marble fireplace. Stella fingered my car keys, lost interest and dropped them on my foot, waved her hands up at the window frames, and babbled *aisle aisle aisle*. I nursed her on the right side. I nursed her on the left side. She slept. I heard how Ward invited Mary Rose to the set to watch him direct a commercial for flavored seltzer – Ward was a director of high-profile commercials that garnered fancy prizes – then, during a break, locked them in the greenroom, where they made love on the linoleum. How he sent Mary Rose not flowers, but slim books whose sole purpose in life was to charm. How he looked her in the eyes when she spoke, instead of around the room or at the spot on the wall just behind her head. How he made her laugh.

'What did the hurricane say to the palm tree? Hold on to your nuts, this is going to be one hell of a blow job.' Mary Rose slapped her thighs, wept with delight.

Oh no.

'In the poem about the rhododendron?' She knuckled the tears out of her eyes with no regard for the hyper-sensitive skin just beneath. She *was* in love. 'He compared my way with shrubs with how I can mend an empty heart.'

'Shouldn't it be fill an empty heart? Or mend a broken heart?' I bounced Stella, even though she was mewing in a way that said, 'Cut it out or I'll shriek.'

'It doesn't matter.'

I just looked at her. I wanted to say, *Mary Rose, it will matter. It will!*

This wasn't entirely true. It will matter, until you have a child, then it won't matter again. Look at me. I have eyes for no one but Stella. I am moved to tears by the thought of Stella's feet, those rosy toes as round as marbles, the soles of her feet like the faces of two little eyeless old men. One time I put her entire foot in my mouth, just to see what it was like. The foot tasted like Stella smelled: Downey, Desitin, and clean baby. I was planning for a day in the future when she would be an eye-rolling teen and accuse me of sticking my foot in my mouth and I would say, 'No, but I stuck your foot in my mouth – when you were about six months old!' Dumb, dumb, dumb beyond belief. But it's one of the wonders and powers of motherhood: It pleases me, so who cares?

'It's ready!' cried Audra, rushing from the kitchen with mincing steps, the kind meant to represent hurry. 'Mary Rose, honey, I hope you can stomach my parsnip and clam stuffing. I've had some people complain that the parsnip is too rooty and the clam is too gooey, but I think they complement each other perfectly. Just like you and Ward.'

I followed Mary Rose into the dining room. To the back of her head I said, 'Rooty and Gooey sitting in a tree, K-I-S-S-I-N-G.' Maybe I am not simply a terrible mother; I may also be a terrible friend.

Mary Rose ignored me, sat where Audra told her to. The walls in the vast dining room and breakfast room were painted with gold leaf that had blistered and buckled in the dampness.

Suddenly, hubbub! Or rather hubbub, Baron style. Little Hank, Ward, and Dicky rolled in, beating their sleeves to warm up, stamping their feet, as if they'd just come in from a dogsled race in a blizzard instead of basketball in the driveway. They behaved like an overzealous amateur theater group given the improvisation *hectic!* causing Audra to rush back into the kitchen to find a corkscrew. One was found. Much to-do about the wine, opening it and pouring it.

'Where's the GD corkscrew?' said Little Hank. 'Dad, did you leave the GD corkscrew on the boat?' Little Hank, in a kelly-green polo shirt and madras slacks, always looked like he'd been beamed up straight from a fraternity kegger, circa 1964.

I got the feeling Little Hank was trying to change the subject, something they'd been talking about before being called in to dinner. Or maybe I was simply projecting, based on what I know about Dicky: *Romeo's Dagger* was the high point of his life, The Big Game meets The One That Got Away, and was a topic he could flog to death. Dicky dropped into his chair. He was wearing a huge blue plaid flannel shirt, exercise pants with stripes up the side. Unlike the other Barons, who were of medium height and build, Dicky was tall and curiously wide. He had hips. Next to his brothers and parents, he looked as if he was gestated next to a nuclear power plant. Chernobyl Dicky, I thought, everything about him big and pink.

'Nowadays a simple life crisis isn't even good enough,' he was saying. He fiddled with the silverware, hit the prongs of the salad fork with one finger and sent it flying into the middle of the table. 'You've also got to be training for the Olympics. Your life has to have a hook, is what I'm saying. The crisis itself isn't even good enough anymore. Do you hear what I'm saying? Who was that little girl in Texas who got stuck in the well and had to have that guy with no collarbone rescue her?

15

That story would never have been made today. Not even for TV.'

'Have another drink, Dick,' said Ward, winking at Little Hank. Little Hank winked back too enthusiastically, grateful to be in on one of Ward's jokes. I sighed. Other people's family dynamics.

Audra brought in a high chair from another room. I assumed it had belonged to her boys, even though it looked too new, with a special nontoxic glaze and padded with a seat cover trimmed with a yellow ruffle. Once Stella was tucked into the chair, she popped a crinkly red thumb into her mouth. When she was unsure of her surroundings she never cried, just became as uninteresting as possible. Maybe she would grow up to be a spy.

Ward pretended to sit in the air right next to Mary Rose, then scooted her over with his hips so he could share the chair with her. 'Not enough chairs, Ma. Guess I'll have to share with Mary Rose.' He wrapped his arms around her arms, laid a photogenic cheekbone on her shoulder. Ward also has one of those forever-boyish forelocks around which decades-long Hollywood careers have been built. What is it about a man with good hair?

Big Hank stood at the head of the table, methodically carving the turkey into disks with an electric carving knife. He hummed like a bored dentist. There was something with the turkey. It was white and shiny. All I could think of was a burn victim. Of course. Roasted without its skin. Audra's devotion to low fat extended even to the calorie-fest of the year. Around the table, bowls were passed: steamed carrots, broccoli, Brussels sprouts, whole-wheat rolls as heavy as billiard balls.

Only in sit-coms do women usually make quips and asides about the god-awful cooking of their hostess. Mostly, we smile and offer compliments; the worse the meal, the more effusive the compliments. I watched Mary Rose take a dry oval of charred bird and try to disguise it with two ladles of gravy, which turned out to be steamed and whipped rutabagas.

'Yum! This is a real taste treat!' said Mary Rose. She put the fork in her mouth, then took it out with the food still on it. 'Mrs. Baron, meant to tell you, before I leave tonight let me take in the calla lilies for you. It's getting a little nippy out there.'

'I'll nippy *you*,' said Ward, walking his fingers up Mary Rose's side in the direction of her breasts.

'Ward.' Mary Rose squirmed, delirious as a fourteen-year-old on her first date.

'Ward! Stop it some more, stop it some more,' said Ward in a girly falsetto.

'For one thing,' continued Dicky, louder, 'everyone wants murder. They prefer multiple murder. What was so good about *Romeo's Dagger* – and it was good Brooke, don't ever forget what a fine job you did there, do you hear what I'm saying? – is that it had meaning. It was about love and courage. It was about more than how twisted people are. Although twisted is what sells. Twisted is money in the bank.'

'Audra, please, call me Audra,' said Audra to Mary Rose. 'I suspect you're right about the calla lilies, and while we're on the subject, I don't think I've told you how much I love *Paraiso Mexicano*. It's absolutely inspired. I've had enough azaleas and rhodies to last me a lifetime. I adore it, and as I recall, not everyone agreed with me.'

'As I recall, Ma, no one agreed with you,' said Little Hank.

'Mary Rose did. She's the only truly creative landscaper in this entire city,' said Audra.

Paraiso Mexicano was Audra's name for the subtropical garden Mary Rose had planted behind the four-car garage. Other gardeners had told Audra what Mary Rose should have: 'Mrs. Baron, you cannot, I repeat, cannot grow bougainvillea in this climate.'

But where there was money – not to mention the beloved's mother – there was always someone to say, 'If you want the impossible, I'll try to give it to you.' Mary Rose built a trellis for the *Bougainvillea sanderiana* against the south side of the garage, dropped some hibiscus and salmon-colored impatiens in the ground, and told Audra to keep her palms and calla lilies in pots, which could then be transferred to the sunroom in the winter.

'It was all your idea, Audra.'

'But you talked me out of the banana tree. That showed determination and vision. Not every landscaper has determination and vision.'

'I was just following your lead,' said Mary Rose. She was anxious, I think, to be both agreeable while at the same time disavowing responsibility for the collection of exotic plants, some shipped from nurseries in Phoenix, that would no doubt be black and limp with rot come spring.

'You're not eating,' said Audra. 'Have you been morning sick?'

You know that silence.

Suddenly, the weather, which no one had noticed for hours, seemed to be inside the room. The applause of rain against the Italian-tile roof. The candles sputtering in the heavy silver holders, victims of unseen drafts. Mary Rose slid a glance at Ward, who kept eating his carrots, sliding them between half-open lips as if he was feeding a parking meter. She said nothing.

I thought I didn't hear this right. I busied myself trying to feed Stella mashed potatoes.

'You're right, Dick,' said Ward. 'The fact-based movie is in decline. *Romeo's Dagger* was great. What did that one review call it? "Shapely and ironic"?'

'That's what I want on my tombstone,' I said.

'What was the last good true story you saw? Dad? What about you?'

Big Hank looked at Ward over his glasses as if he were mad. 'The last time I was in a theater they still had ushers.' 'This is ridiculous,' said Audra. 'I know you young people talk about everything. For God's sake, look what they advertise on television these days. So let's not stand on ceremony. Yes, Mary Rose, Ward told us the news. And we are thrilled, absolutely thrilled. This is ridiculous. I think we should be honest. I'm beyond thrilled. I thought I was never going to have any grandchildren. And since we're being honest, I might as well say it. Two healthy kids like you and Ward. I'm not racist. You know that about me. But with all those poor African-American girls having a dozen children or more, why, we have to hold up our end, don't we? Us poor old middle-class white people?'

'Speaking of which, who is someone who's never been mugged?'

'Ward, quit trying to change the subject,' said Audra. 'But there's one thing. And I hope you hear me on this, Mary Rose. I know you're kind of the earthy type, and will probably be into all that modern-day homeopathic nonsense, but please, *please*, I beg of you. I've heard of women saving their placentas – good God, how far we've come! Talking about placentas at the dinner table –'

'You're the only one talking about them,' Ward said into his Brussels sprouts. 'And, yes, I would like to change the subject.'

'You little devil,' said Little Hank, pitching a roll across the table.

'Don't interrupt – my *point* is that I do not, I repeat, do not, want you saving the placenta to fertilize the roses. I've heard of that happening. I will absolutely not have your placenta decomposing, or whatever it does, under my "Billy Graham" or "Melodie Parfumee". Mrs. Eldon's daughter-in-law froze her placenta, then when it was time to use it to plant under a tree or something, it wouldn't come out of the Tupperware –'

'Mother! You've made your point!'

'And she had to microwave it. Ward, I'm just trying to show you I'm modern, and that I support you.'

'We understand, Mrs. Baron,' said Mary Rose, tucking her hair behind her ears.

'Please, call me Audra!'

Mary Rose looked at Ward, who was busily smearing whipped rutabaga on a pile of curling meat. He smiled a weak, closed-mouth smile, gave his shoulders a little shrug. 'The answer is: a liberal. To the question, Who is someone who's never been mugged?'

Mary Rose cleared her throat. 'I know you're family and have every right to know, Audra, but we had originally planned on keeping it to ourselves. Until we've had time to adjust.'

Audra giggled, clapped her hands together under her chin. This was easily the most amusing thing she'd heard in ages. 'Mary Rose, you are so adorable. There's no adjusting. Don't you know that? I still look at these boys and say to myself, "I can't believe *you* came out of me." '

2

For a woman, the true advantage of marriage is not having regular sex, but having an on-site partner with whom to debrief. In this day and age anyone can get laid; try finding someone who'll listen to dish at midnight. Before Lyle discovered Realm of the Elf, he was just such a man.

I was eager to get home after Thanksgiving dinner. Wait until Lyle heard about Ward Baron and The Last Living Valkyrie. Lyle does a great improvisational chromosomal analysis, wherein he imagines both the best baby and the worst baby two people could possibly produce. Of the offspring of a software mogul and a runway model he might say: *What if the baby gets his height and her math skills! His lips and hips and her sense of the absurd!* We entertained ourselves for hours with this when Stella was gestating, and haven't laughed so hard since. Then she was born, and was completely herself, and made fools of us both.

I managed to successfully transfer a sleeping Stella from her car seat to her crib without waking her, then tromped down to the basement stairs to Lyle's Lair. A previous owner had had a Space Odyssey decor in mind: The basement walls and unfinished ceiling were spray-painted silver. Lyle had his computer set up against one of the silver walls, on a big square of old dog-brown shag. Next to the computer was a futon, one that has been passed from soon-to-be-married friend to soon-to-be-married friend, until it wound up in Lyle's Lair. Itchy Sister, our thirteen-year-old Rhodesian Ridgeback, sleeps on the futon, where she snores and silently, endlessly farts. On top of the computer Lyle always burns an aromatherapy candle, Seduction, to combat the odor.

'You won't believe this one,' I said to the back of Lyle's head. 'Mary Rose and Ward are an item. Not just an item, but an expectant item.'

I am an expert on the back of my husband's head. Like a character in an experimental play, I talk to it all the time. Lyle's hair is cut by an envious, straight-haired stylist to emphasize his cherubic curls. His best ones – shiny, self-assured – are just to the right of the crown. To the left, they can't decide if they want to be curls or waves. There are four gray hairs, and a black mole on the back of his neck I will one day have to pester him to have checked, if our marriage survives his passion for Realm of the Elf.

'Uh-huh,' he said.

'We can talk about this later,' I said, and started to walk away.

'I'm listening. I'm always listening to you. Uh-oh, now I'm really not feeling well.' He sat forward, attacked the keyboard. Mozart on a particularly frenzied day.

'Do you have a headache? Have you eaten anything?'

'I just got my arm cut off.'

I stared over his shoulder, feigning interest. Realm of the Elf was one of those online role-playing games where you create the persona of some magical Hobbit-like creature, then go around getting mortally wounded in imaginary sword fights and finding precious gems in the virtual bushes. I will never understand the appeal of this or any other text-file computer game. White letters scrolling up a black screen, a cyber ticker tape.

22

I read, 'A marauding troll has just malevolently and with vim chopped off your arm! Your hand is being eaten by deadly acid. Otherwise your soul is full of life. He takes a misshapen trunk from your dove gray pack. Your neck wounds look better.'

'And people say screenplays are poorly written.' I wanted to say, *I'm worried about you! Can't you be into bondage or something more normally deviant?*

He said nothing. Tap-tap-tap-tap-tap. 'I'm just . . . about' Tap-tap-tap-tap-tap.

'I don't know how you can read this stuff hour after hour.'

I sighed, went over and petted Itchy Sister behind an ear. Her black lips turn up at the corners when she gets some attention, even in her sleep.

'Mary Rose and Ward are going to have a baby!' I told the back of his head.

'Let me just see if I can find someone to get my arm on, and I'll be right with you. There's a healer in the next village who owes me a favor.'

I went upstairs to check on Stella, then went to bed.

A week after Thanksgiving, when I arrived at Mary Rose's house with Stella to watch the Knicks versus the Blazers, Mary Rose wasn't home. Like many people in our city, Mary Rose and I never missed a basketball game. Our city endured drippy falls, drenched winters, drizzly springs, and no Major League teams save basketball, which made for a civic fanaticism rivaling that of the rampaging hordes who follow soccer in Europe. Mary Rose and I pitched in for a special cable package – not cheap – that broadcasted all home games that weren't carried on network television. When a game was carried only on radio, we huddled around Mary Rose's boom box, set in the middle of her coffee table, like would-be war widows listening for news from the front. Mary Rose would undercook a frozen pizza. Sometimes I brought an aluminum tray of take-out nachos.

Mary Rose lived in a bile-green bungalow that had been converted into a triplex, in a part of the city where the streets were lined with old Victorians groaning on tiny lots. It was the homeliest house on the block, but Mary Rose had a deal with the landlord. Mr. D'Addio gave her a break in the rent in exchange for her mowing the lawn and keeping the sidewalk free of the smashed plums that fell from the three ornamental trees that grew on the parking strip. The plums, while beautiful, were a nuisance. They stained the pavement a bloody maroon, as well as attracted a ferocious species of wasp that could sting you through your shoe.

I stood in the entryway of the triplex, talking to apricot-haired Mrs. Wanamaker, who lived in the unit downstairs. The entryway smelled of wet dog and the perfume inserts of magazines. Mrs. Wanamaker was fascinated to hear about Stella's affection for avocados and taking off her own diaper. She also admired Stella's black-and-red Blazer jump suit. The true mates of this world are not husbands and wives, but lonely old women and exhausted young mothers.

Mary Rose bounded up the front steps, apologized for being late. First, there was Mrs. Marsh, wanting all her dahlia bulbs dug up for the winter, then Hot Lips pizza lost her order.

'Pepperoni double cheese,' she said, flying the cardboard box over my head as she jogged past me up the stairs. So much energy for someone newly pregnant, I thought.

I dragged myself upstairs behind her, Stella's car seat banging against my shins, the strap of her diaper bag cutting into my shoulder. My knees ached. Once inside, I dropped the bag – twice as heavy as the Perfect Wonderment herself – stuffed to the gills with powders, ointments and sunscreens, Q-Tips and mittens, a change of clothes, rattles and teething toys, books for several different age levels (in the event she started to read while away from home and proved to be a genius), and a half-dozen empty plastic bottles, designed in Denmark according to some enlightened Scandinavian feeding principle, lint stuck to the milk-encrusted nipple.

'If I have one piece of advice for the woman looking to get pregnant, it's train for a decathlon,' I said. 'It's amazing to me how everyone always wants to help a pregnant woman, when the baby is all nice and tucked away in utero, but then once the kid is born, and your life as a schlepper begins in earnest, no one thinks to lend you a hand.'

'Was I supposed to help you?' said Mary Rose. 'I didn't know I was supposed to help you. You always seem like you've got everything under control.' Mary Rose set the pizza in the middle of the coffee table, then glanced around the living room to make sure there was nothing Stella could get into. Stella wasn't crawling yet. She sat where you put her. Nevertheless, Mary Rose was under the impression that a baby, once freed from the confines of the womb, was biologically programmed to seek disaster, compelled to stick her fingers into sockets, choke on a dusty bead found beneath the couch.

Even if this were true, a baby would be completely safe at Mary Rose's. The only time Ward had ever ventured upstairs, according to Mary Rose, he'd said that if Mowers and Rakers didn't work out, Mary Rose could always get a job doing interior design for a monastery. The living room was tiny, the walls toffee-colored with three windows on one side. Opposite the windows were two doors, one that gave off onto the front hallway, the other to the back hallway that lead to the kitchen and the huge bathroom which, due to the architectural gymnastics involved in the conversion from charming house to funky triplex, was bigger than the living room. There was nothing on the walls.

Acquisitive Ward, he of the Arts and Crafts-style living room set, collection of vintage neon beer signs, and three complete sets of Fiesta Ware, jokingly (or maybe not, Ward had a way of saying things that were more hurtful than funny, then tried to pass the insult off as a joke when you got annoyed) said her spare quarters were an affectation.

'He accused me of being self-consciously minimalist,' said Mary Rose. 'I told him it was called "the less you had, the less you had to clean." I'm not a minimalist, I'm *practical*.' Like everyone newly in love, she reported this humdrum exchange with pride and astonishment, as if to say, See how we know each other? See how we tease each other? Already, it's come to that.

I felt a prick of irritation. Before I could trace it to its roots I said, 'Practical, unless you count having a baby with a man you hardly know.' That sounded meaner than I meant it to. I backpedaled. 'I mean, not that *knowing* the man you have your baby with makes any difference. Actually, maybe knowing the father is worse. Then you don't have any excuse for perpetuating his genes.' I was starting to go off. I laughed too loud, startling Stella.

Mary Rose retrieved her backpack from where it hung on the hall-closet doorknob, then fished around inside. 'Look at this.'

It was a handout given her by Dr. Vertamini, her OB/GYN. A list of symptoms that signal impending miscarriage: pain or burning on urination; vaginal spotting or bleeding; leaking or gushing fluid from vagina; uterine contractions; severe nausea; severe vomiting; abdominal pain; dizziness or light-headedness; severe headache; swelling of face, eyes, fingers, or toes; blurred eyesight; reduced fetal movement; absence of fetal movement for twenty-four hours (from the twenty-eighth week of pregnancy on).

'What do you think it means by pain, exactly?' asked Mary Rose.

'Are you experiencing any pain?'

'No. I figured it has to do with malpractice laws or something. Dr. Vertamini probably gives one of these to everyone, don't you think? She just didn't print it up for me.'

'Oh, no, I think she printed it up just for you.'

'So I shouldn't worry, is what you're saying.' Mary Rose manufactured a smile. Her teeth looked like bathroom tile installed by a perfectionist.

'Get used to worrying is more like it. You'll get past the first trimester, then there's the second, then the third, then the birth. No sooner is the baby born then you start worrying about can she hear all right? Is she retarded? And this new thing I read in the paper. Children who *don't* go to day care have a higher rate of leukemia. Children who *do* go to day care wind up sociopaths. It's a prison sentence of worry. No parole.'

Mary Rose dropped the handout on the table, dragged a slice of pizza from the box, pinching off swags of cheese with her long, nail-bitten fingers. I got the feeling she didn't like my answer. Or maybe just my sermonizing. I do have a tendency to go on a bit. But she knows this about me, so why did she bother asking?

'What was all that business at Thanksgiving with Dicky?' she asked abruptly. 'I asked Ward, and he just rolled his eyes.'

'Poor old Dicky. It would kill him that you didn't know all about it.'

I was happy to get off the subject of motherhood and told Mary Rose probably more than she wanted to know about poor Jennifer Allen, whom Dicky had fallen in love with when he was at U.S.C. They became acquainted because they were both from our city, had gone to rival private high schools. She had a head of sunny curls that compensated for all of her

27

shortcomings. Jennifer and Dicky loved each other in the dedicated, impractical way of the well-off. He bought her a yellow Vespa for her birthday. She convinced her parents to allow Dicky to accompany them on their annual two-week Christmas pilgrimage to St. Croix.

After two terms at school, Jennifer got sick. Or it was presumed she was sick. She began falling asleep in class. She was pale as a mushroom. It was all those weekend ski trips to Mammoth those late nights with Dicky, the midterms, beer bongs, glee clubs. It was the anemia typical of the earnest, nutritionally ignorant vegan whose idea of saving the planet involves subsisting on a diet of Coke Classic and Cool Ranch Doritos. All Jennifer Allen really needed was a vacation from being a nineteen-year-old college student with no worries, but because all this collegiate carrying-on is presumed to be a normal upper-middle-class child's birthright, nobody thought anything of it.

When Jennifer came home for the summer, her mother took her to one of our city's most well-respected specialists, where she was diagnosed with a rare, aggressive form of cancer: leukemic reticuloendotheliosis, also known as hairy cell leukemia. It had already invaded her marrow, spleen, and blood.

The shock felt by Dicky Baron and Jennifer Allen almost stopped their young hearts there and then. Who had ever heard of such a thing? Hairy cell leukemia. How could something so ridiculous-sounding be fatal? If she chose to accept treatment, there would be useless operations, followed by a round of expensive, nausea-producing chemotherapy that would not, in the end, postpone a death both painful and tedious. In the meantime, it would spell the end of the sunny curls. It would mean a life of valiant hat wearing.

Jennifer wept. There was not much hope. There was, however, the romance of dying while you were still young and pretty, featuring the interesting delusion that you can some how experience the benefits of death without actually ceasing to exist. One day, while Dicky and Jennifer were alone in the house, Dicky found Big Hank's .45 semi-automatic while he was going through Father's bedside table, looking for something interesting to pinch. Dicky and Jennifer believed it was fate.

Dicky gave the gun to Jennifer, clicking off the safety and turning his back, as if she were a stranger about to get undressed.

Dicky's comment, when he was arraigned on charges of manslaughter, was, 'I thought there would be more noise and less blood.' The detective in charge of the investigation wore rubbers over his tasseled loafers and was glad of it. Even the ceiling needed to be repainted.

In *Romeo's Dagger*, the first of the three movies I've managed to get off the ground, I insisted that Jennifer shoot herself off screen. We have all seen enough, I said. We have proved to ourselves and the world that the American people are unflinching. All has been told; all has been shown. I made an impassioned plea to the studio for the power of restraint. When that didn't work, I cited the shower sequence in the original *Psycho*. I got my way. Now that I have Stella, I am relieved on behalf of Jennifer Allen's mother.

Dicky maintained throughout the trial that if he and Jennifer had done anything wrong, it was in telling her parents. If Jennifer had been less conscientious, she never would have complained to her mother, and no doctors would have been involved. No medical clerks would have been involved, medical clerks who make clerical errors.

For Jennifer Allen, his Jennifer Allen, did not have hairy cell leukemia. Her chart had been confused with that of another Jennifer Allen by Corrine Clingenpeel, a medical receptionist trying to hold down two jobs, raise her young son, and get through nursing school. It was a single-mother mistake, as the papers were fond of reporting, the mistake of a woman overwhelmed. For this Jennifer Allen, Dicky's Jennifer Allen, was the healthiest person on which an autopsy had ever been performed in the state, according to our city's chief coroner.

It made the national news, and the nation was duly outraged. An investigation into hospital filing systems was opened up. Briefly, the blame was laid at the smelly feet of a cadre of sixteen-year-old computer hackers. For several weeks the nightly news ran stories about people who had gone in for knee surgery and had their gall bladders removed instead. Dicky ('looking not unlike the young Nick Nolte' – Associated Press) wept on all three networks, plus CNN. He was tried, acquitted, and signed by William Morris.

I'd been rattling around the film industry for six years when Audra brought me the rights to Dicky's side of the story. In Hollywood there are always several sides for sale. I was in the art department on a feature at the time. For twelve hours a day I moved furniture on, off, and around the set. The movie was set in Victorian times and all the highboys, chiffonniers, and sideboards were made of solid oak and cherry. I wore a kidney belt and a look of perpetual self-pity. I liked movies. If I liked moving furniture I would have gotten a job with Bekins. At this time Dicky's case came to trial, and an article about Jennifer Allen's death appeared as a *Newsweek* cover story.

When Jennifer Allen's parents changed their phone number, the better to discourage all interest in their daughter's unfortunate death, Audra was besieged. For several weeks it seemed everyone who had ever entertained the notion of producing a movie wanted to buy the rights to Dicky's version of events.

But Audra Baron comes from a long line of implacable

Vermont dairy farmers on one side and crafty Polish petit bourgeois politicians on the other. She also was a devotee of *Entertainment Tonight*. In other words, she was not impressed with their urgings and entreaties, with the videotapes they overnight expressed to her as a sample of their work, the trouble, time, and money they took to fly up and visit her in person.

She trusted none of them and called me, bi-weekly becoming daily becoming hourly, to make sure she was doing the right thing. I do not remember exactly how it happened, but suddenly Audra began referring people to me. 'Talk to my niece Brooke. She is handling the rights.' That my only credentials for pulling off this task were my stint in the art department as a beast of burden seemed not to bother Audra. I was better than a stranger, although I practically was one. She insisted I call her Aunt.

It was a time in Hollywood when the edgy, Italian-suited, business-school-educated studio clone was on the way out, and no one knew what was on the way in. All anyone could be sure of was that the creative elite had stopped washing their hair. A-list directors began showing up for meetings looking like earnest philosophy majors. They wore sweaters with holes in the elbows and smelled.

I didn't know any of this. I didn't know anything. I didn't know enough to call myself a producer. I returned all my phone calls at the first opportunity, ate lunch at home – peanut butter and jelly on whole-wheat toast with half an apple. I was on time for my meetings, wore job-interview clothes, and never offered anything I couldn't deliver. I didn't negotiate. I said: 'I've got the story of Jennifer Allen's death, from the point of view of her boyfriend. Take it or leave it.'

If they left it I went somewhere else, in my 1979 Datsun with no car phone. When I took the project elsewhere, I presumed I was really taking it elsewhere, unaware this was a negotiating tactic. When the studio I had left called back and offered more money, more control, I said: 'No. I'm sorry. I'm already talking to someone else. Thank you anyway.'

No one had ever heard of such a thing. No one knew what to make of me. I was so middle-class, so resolutely un-shrewd, un-feisty, un-iconoclastic, un-all-those-other-adjectives used to describe brash up-and-comers that I was perceived as being shrewd, feisty, and iconoclastic.

For a few weeks, everyone wanted to have a meeting with me just so they could tell their friends and associates how I never *once* said *Romeo's Dagger* was a cross between this box-office smash and that critically acclaimed success; how I drank Dr Pepper and ate club sandwiches and seemed not to be watching my weight. My brand-new agent Melissa Lee Rottock performed the necessary arm-twisting and obscenity-slinging, and together we were able to get a deal set before people got bored with my style of doing business, which was no style at all.

'In Dicky's defense, I have to say that it was a pretty heady time. For all of us. But then, you know, we made the movie and moved on. But he's never gotten over not being famous anymore. I think he even goes to a support group of other people who were also famous for something or other. There's that Olympic athlete who got shot in the groin during a domestic squabble, and a chicken rancher who landed a 747 when the pilot had a stroke. On the set, we joked – it was cruel, I have to admit – that Dicky was already planning his next career move. Trying to figure out a way to deliver a set of quintuplets in the middle of a hurricane or unwittingly discover the gene for obesity.'

'Also, of course, in the middle of a hurricane,' said Mary Rose. 'Preferably the worst one in a hundred years.'

'Now you've got it.'

Mary Rose got up and turned on the tube; the game was a minute into the first quarter. We sat together in the dark on Mary Rose's sleeper sofa, a Goodwill reject of nubby brown polyester fabric whose seat yawned open, jawlike, when no one was sitting on it. Stella dozed in my lap. The furnace kicked on. Outside there was the occasional roar of sudden rain.

We watched while Ajax Green, the star of our team, missed both of his free throws.

'One guy starts missing, then they all start missing,' I said.

'They don't want one guy to feel like a loser all alone, so they all join in,' said Mary Rose.

'Here's my prescription for the off-season: group therapy in the morning, free-throw practice in the afternoon.'

'The other reason they don't make their free throws is because it's a *free* throw. They don't feel like they deserve anything that's free. They only feel happy overcoming a ten-point deficit with seven seconds left to play. They only feel happy if their situation is completely impossible,' said Mary Rose. 'There's Derik Crawshaw though. He seems relatively well-adjusted.'

'Yeah, but he's new.'

We could go on like this all night, and often did. We thought we might be transverbalists: women who enjoyed not cross-dressing, but cross-talking, talking like men.

By the end of the first quarter Stella was awake and fussing, the Blazers were down by four, and Ward Baron had decided to stop by.

Stopping by was not something Mary Rose generally approved of. People who knew Mary Rose did not drop by. Whenever I waxed nostalgic about college, during which time I shared a huge old house with five other people, all of whom had issued open invitations for everyone they knew to crash whenever they wanted to, Mary Rose's pupils dilated with anxiety. Needless to say with Ward, it was a different story altogether. At least a first.

Ward and I had an odd relationship. He reminded me of Lyle: lanky, with unkempt brown curls and a deep voice that cracked with emotion at will, the compulsion to tell dumb jokes. When we were teenagers the Barons came to California to stay for a month with us in our rented beach house at Corona del Mar. Ward and I were on the verge of getting one of those cousin things going that are a familiar staple of ninteenth-century English literature, but we were both shy, and I was neither large enough nor hardy enough for his tastes. He fell for a five-foot-eleven sailing instructor instead.

So there were murky feelings swirling around our relationship even before *Romeo's Dagger*. Ward wanted me to hire him to direct. He thought, perhaps rightly so, that his mother had given me my break, so I should give him his. As savvy as Ward imagines himself to be, he thought what all people who are not in the movie business think: that a producer is like the immigrant owner of a Vietnamese restaurant who has a job for every family member who wants one. In truth, the most powerful person involved in the production, in this case the cuddly cute comedian R—, who (in his first serious role) played Dicky Baron, got to pad the crew with as many family members, chefs, and favorite kung fu instructors as he wanted. Likewise, cuddly cute R— had his pick of the litter, director-wise. But Ward was persistent. He thought, as men typically do, that I could be softened up, worn down, stone-washed, whatever. First, he tried to appeal to my cousinly instincts, sending me pictures of Audra and Big Hank vacationing in Milan along with a copy of his director's reel. When that didn't work, he came to L.A. and took me to dinner at the beach, hoping the salt air and overcooked swordfish would rekindle our romance *manqué* of twenty years earlier.

When that didn't work out, he resorted to good-natured bullying.

'You don't know how many people would sell – well, maybe not their souls, but their houses in Montana! – to work with me. Who's executive producing this thing, anyway?' he said.

'I am,' I said. It was a lie, but he was getting on my nerves. 'Anyway, I've showed your reel to R— and he thinks you're too slick.'

'You mean stylized,' he said.

'I mean facile,' I said.

'Perfect, then, for your movie,' he said.

'Hiya, baby,' he said now, to Mary Rose. Ward moved closer to kiss her cheek, then made a last-minute detour and swooped down to plant a peck on her brown wool sweater in the region of her belly button. He wore one of those enormous black leather jackets that crackled with every breath. 'Oh, and hello to you too, Mary Rose.'

Ward scooted Mary Rose over, and the four of us sat squashed on the couch, like people on a lifeboat. Ward gently placed a Styrofoam take-out carton on Mary Rose's lap. 'I remember you liked these.'

Mary Rose clapped her hands over her heart and sighed, 'Oh.' Ward's hair curled over his collar. She reached up, almost shyly, and combed it with her fingers. He closed his eyes, let his head drop back into the palm of her hand. I watched this out of the corner of my eye – it was really very sweet – when suddenly Mary Rose yanked her hand out from under Ward's head, which snapped forward like that of a crash test dummy. The Styrofoam container slid to the floor and popped open.

'Oh, come on!' yelled Mary Rose. She gestured at the TV. 'Where I come from, getting your mouth guard knocked halfway across the floor is a foul.'

'Baby, franchise players never foul,' said Ward.

'What are you talking about, sweetheart? Pippen's got two,' said Mary Rose. 'Everyone else has *four*. Guys coming in off the bench get called for tucking in their shirts.'

'My point exactly, sweetie.'

Then Mary Rose spied the container on the floor, inside the square white clam was a handful of pale brown cookies. She leaned forward, peered closer. 'What are those?'

'Peanut-butter cookies. Left over from the shoot. I remembered they were your favorite.'

Mary Rose cupped one long hand over the other, continued to peer down at the cookies as if they were some poisonous animal devouring its prey, interesting to watch but lethal to touch. 'Not *my* favorite.'

'Since when? Is this some kind of pregnancy food thing?' Ward looked at me and rolled his eyes.

'She's allergic to peanuts,' I said.

'You are? You never told me that. Why didn't you ever tell me that? I would never have brought these, if . . .' He leaned over and snapped the Styrofoam case shut, as if the mere sight of them might cause Mary Rose to go into anaphylactic shock. 'I must be thinking of the ex-wife.'

'You have an ex-wife?'

Ward was silent. He popped the container open again, then snapped it shut. Open, shut, open, shut. 'How can you tell your husband is dead? The sex is the same, but you get the remote.'

'You never told me you have an ex-wife.'

'You never told me you were allergic to peanuts.'

We all turned our attention to a free-throw shot. We watched, rapt, as the ball twirled around the rim. Lynne Baron! I'd forgotten about her. She and Ward were just separated when he and I had our acrimonious overcooked swordfish dinner. She did something in the movies. I remember, because he told me she was getting out of the film business and into training Seeing Eye dogs. 'She wanted to get out of the blind leading the blind and into Labrador retrievers leading the blind,' he'd said. Then I remembered: She'd been a Frederick's of Hollywood lingerie model who threw in the thong to become a food designer. She was well-known in food-design circles. She did for a plate of deepfried Cajun jumbo shrimp what the makeup artist, hair stylist, and wardrobe consultant did for the actress eating it.

I must confess, I then did something very unfriendlike. I gloated. This, Mary Rose, *this* is why you don't get pregnant with someone you've just met. If you want a joint project, build a gazebo, learn to swing dance, but don't, *don't* have a baby. I felt wise, suddenly, instead of like the judgmental curmudgeon I knew myself to be.

When Ward excused himself to use the bathroom, I told Mary Rose, 'Ask to talk to him outside. Don't let him get away with this. You deserve some answers. You deserve them *now*. Don't give him a chance to put together a good story. That's what men do, you know, say nothing until they have a chance to put together a story.'

'I know,' said Mary Rose. 'I know about men.'

'Well, clearly you don't,' I said, 'or not about this one, anyway.'

Mary Rose zapped me with a glare that could cause radiation burns, but when Ward came back, she asked to speak with him outside.

A deck ran along the front of the house and could be reached only through Mary Rose's bedroom, a cramped space with no insulation, big enough only for a double bed and the upended orange crate that served as a nightstand.

The rain had let up. Mary Rose sat in one of the rickety white plastic patio chairs, put her feet up on one of her window boxes. A huge parsley plant colonized one of the boxes. The other was a wasteland of twine-colored petunias that had long ago gone to seed. She left the door open. I hit the mute button on the remote, so I could hear everything.

Ward stood. 'I should have told you about Lynne. I should have, but this all happened so fast and I never think of her. She never crosses my mind. You're the only woman who crosses me.'

'Crosses your mind, you mean. So how long were you married?'

'Long enough to know it wasn't going to work.'

'And that would be . . .'

'Fifteen months.'

'But who's counting, huh?'

'You have to make it difficult on me, don't you? I said I was sorry. I am sorry. I'm a schmuck, I admit it. I have an ex-wife, all right? But we were over long before I met you.'

'How long?'

'Over a year.'

'What happened? To the marriage, I mean.'

'I wanted kids, she didn't. We argued. She had an affair. We grew apart.'

'Wow, that just about covers all the bases, doesn't it?'

'I love you, Mary Rose. I love our baby. My mother and father, we all love this baby.'

I suspect it may have been the inclusion of Audra and Big Hank in this love fest, but something made Mary Rose say something odd and, even to my ears, ambiguous. 'There is no baby, Ward.'

Later, when she was telling me her version of events, she said that what she meant was, 'I saw our baby in the ultrasound, and it's not a baby, but a tiny, pulsing bean with seashell ears and a gentle Martian face.' What she meant was, It's not a baby *per se*. It's a He-bean (she was already certain the bean was a boy).

38

Ward wet his lips. 'You got an abortion?'

Mary Rose said nothing. She leaned forward and tugged out one of the dead petunias.

'You should have told me. I know it's your body and all that bullshit, but I *am* the father. There's half of me in there. It's not just you.'

'Why didn't you ever tell me you were married before?'

'This will kill my parents. I hope you know that.'

Suddenly, he picked up one of the patio chairs and chucked it off the deck. It bounced down the front walk, coming to rest on the sidewalk, beneath the ornamental plums. 'They were really looking forward to our having this baby.'

'I understand, Ward. There's just one thing. *We're* not having this baby. I am.'

'You said you got an abortion,' said Ward.

'You did,' said Mary Rose. 'I meant that it's still technically a fetus, not even that. An embryo, really. It's far from being a baby yet, is what I meant. You jumped to conclusions.'

Ward looked over the railing as though suddenly interested in the fate of the eight-dollar patio chair. 'Let's just forget this and start the evening over, can we?'

She let him kiss her. I watched though the doorway.

I'm not convinced that Mary Rose wanted to forget about any of it. I think what she really wanted at that moment was to call a time-out. She wanted the gestation of the He-bean to freeze so that she could think things over. But in making the choice to have the child, Mary Rose had sacrificed time-outs forever. Next to gravity, bearing a child is the modern world's last unalterable fact. Marriages are easily dissolved, morality readily ignored, laws circumvented; an operation can be had to give a boy a vagina or a girl a penis. A fetus cares not whether its mother and father have argued; it cares not that you have lost your job, that the economy has collapsed, that you have been stricken with the flu. On it comes.

I'm guessing, but I imagine it was the knowledge that on or about June 12, Mary Rose would be having Ward's baby, or so she thought, that urged Mary Rose to give Ward the benefit of the doubt. Lynne or no Lynne.

Either that, or she was a fool. Strike that. Who am I to talk?

3

One day in early December I bumped into Audra at our city's
most prosperous health food store, where you can buy seven
different types of organically produced chutney but are looked
upon with scorn if you happen to need a simple can of green
beans. The winter rain had set in for good. Any flirting with
crisp, late-fall weather was over; nature had had her way with
us. It would now rain for months, never varying in intensity or
degree from day to day. As a suicide-prevention technique,
newscasters kept claiming we needed the water.

The store also carried expensive organic potato chips,
which, once inside your mouth, broke into unpleasant
gum-stabbing slivers. I had stopped here on my way home
from the Children's Indoor Play Gym to pick up a bag of these
to eat during Stella's next nap. If I took time to drive to the
regular supermarket for the less expensive, periodontally
friendly chips, Stella would fall asleep in the car. If she fell
asleep in the car, she would not take a nap when we got home.
Why a five-minute catnap in the car prevented a ninety-
minute snooze in her crib was a mystery, and would remain
one throughout her infanthood.

By the cash registers was a large notions section where you
could buy scented candles, woven Guatemalan bracelets,
water-purifying systems, books on everything from organic

farming to curing candida, watercolor greeting cards by local artists, and an assortment of tie-dye.

As I staggered up to get in line, chips in one hand, Stella leaning away from me to grab a whisk hanging from a hook in the other, I saw Audra.

She was holding up a small hot-pink tie-dyed T-shirt, her fox-eyed gaze fastened on a point past the registers, past the wire rack stacked with alternative newspapers, past the uncertain present and into the phantasmagorical future, where she was struggling to calculate the size her unborn grandchild would be a year from now. She was dressed in a pleated denim skirt, white turtleneck patterned with tiny acorns, penny loafers, and pantyhose. Audra's head shot up at the sound of Stella's babbling. 'Oh, my, and who have we here? Do you smile? Are you a smiler? Aren't you a stunning brute?'

She didn't see me. No one does, of course. Being the mother of a beautiful baby is the next best thing to being in the Witness Relocation Program. This was my chance. I could have, should have, turned my head, slunk away. I didn't think I wanted to get into it with Audra. I was afraid we would fall into talking about Mary Rose, and as much as I felt the need to ask someone – rhetorically, of course – what in the hell Mary Rose thought she was doing, dishing with Audra would be a betrayal.

'You remember Stella,' I said. 'Hi, Audra.'

She looked not at all surprised to see me. 'You know, I didn't realize until Thanksgiving that you and Mary Rose were such good friends.'

Audra had a way of saying things to which there was no response. I bounced Stella on my hip, something I did when I was nervous. 'Yup. Even went to different high schools together.'

'So you're best friends, then. Tell-each-other-everything kind of friends.'

'I guess so.'

She asked nothing about me, not how I'd been, nor what I was up to. Audra was incurious about anything that didn't affect her directly, a trait the rich share with the toddler. Still, I always felt I owed her. She gave me my start, and my stop: I saved some money from *Romeo's Dagger* and another film I did right after it – the one directed by the twins, set in the Yukon – so that when I finally had a child, I could take a year off to be with my kid. I couldn't escape the feeling I had Audra to thank for this.

Audra held the tie-dyed T-shirt on the palm of her hand. 'This is for my grandbaby. Is it cute or bizarre? I can't decide.' She peered at the stitching along the neck. 'I seem to have to buy everything I lay eyes on. Was it like that for your mother with this one?'

'My mother's idea of the perfect baby present was a three-year supply of baby wipes, which, of course, *is* the perfect baby present, but it's not very romantic. Then, neither is having a baby, I guess.'

'But I should indulge the urge now, don't you think? I don't think Mary Rose appreciates my interest, but this child is my flesh and blood too, isn't she? My attorney assures me there's such a thing these days as grandparents' rights.'

'Of course,' I said, moving to pat her forearm, forgetting I had no hand to pat it with. I wagged my elbow in her direction.

'I don't imagine she'll let me help much with the wedding, either. I know she lost her own mother when she was very young. So you'd think . . .'

'Absolutely . . .' I said. What wedding? Mary Rose and Ward? Only a week earlier he was lying to her about his ex-wife and hurling patio furniture over the deck railing, and now they were getting married? Of course. The laws of the physics of love dictate that for every unpleasant furniture-hurling argument there is an equal and opposite delirious sheet-twisting, headboard-thumping reconciliation. This one apparently included a marriage proposal as well.

'I think a baby needs two parents,' Audra continued. 'I don't go for all these women in their thirties just deciding to go ahead and have a baby on their own.'

'True. It's much better to have an audience watch you do all the work,' I said.

Audra looked at me blankly, then laughed. 'I forgot you were funny.'

She wound up buying the T-shirt in hot pink, turquoise, yellow, and multi. Tossed in a few board books for good measure. Also, a silver teething ring.

I left without buying anything, had suddenly lost my appetite for the organic gum-stabbing chips, knew it was a waste of money anyway. Stella had snatched a loofah from the bath display and I wrenched it from her grip. She looked shocked, opened her mouth in preparation of a scream.

Getting Stella into her car seat day in, day out was starting to make me feel as if I were part of some army special forces training program. I performed a moderate deep-knee bend – *crickle crackle pop* – unlocked the car door, ground down into a full deep-knee bend in order to release the lever that allowed the front seat to flip forward with a *thropp!*, then raised myself up just until I felt my thighs quiver – tell me some Olympic alpine ski team could not benefit from this – at the same time bending forward into the backseat while resting my chin on the roof. Only when I felt as if I was in a position that would give Houdini déjà vu did I blindly drop the jitterbugging Stella into her car seat. Of course, I couldn't see a thing, because Stella had pulled my hood down over my eyes.

It was raining. My feet were soaked. I got in the car, slammed the hem of my jacket in the door. Stella, I could tell from the ripe smell, had a project. I felt, suddenly, like a prisoner on a chain gang. Do they have chain gangs anymore? Or is it considered cruel and unusual punishment? They still have motherhood, and fifteen-pound near-toddlers with dirty diapers who need to be hauled around. No one's seen fit to call that cruel and unusual, I noticed.

Stella had a cry that sounded like a cross between an opera star in deep mourning and an engine that wouldn't start. Aaanh-aaanh-aaanh-aaanh-*AAANH!* Aaanh-aaanh-aaanh-aaanh-*AAANH!*

'Stella, stop it! Stop it! Shut *up!*' I covered my ears with my hands. Even then it seemed overdramatic, but there you go.

This wasn't the worst of it, telling my precious, my dearest, to shut up for no good reason other than my feet were wet and I had lost my patience. I hated to admit it, but I agreed with Audra. How square is that? It does takes two people to raise a child. Actually, I agreed with Hillary Clinton even more. It takes a village, a village of grandmothers willing to use a Gold Card to buy a wardrobe of cheaply made baby T-shirts that the child would outgrow after wearing each of them exactly once. It took the village treasury.

I felt myself getting teary-eyed, told myself to knock it off, which only made me feel worse. While being with a child may make you young again, allowing you to experience the world through a child's perceptions – have the burnished, catcher's mitt-sized maple leaves of autumn ever seemed so splendid? When was singing ever so much fun? Yawning, belching, the swamp like gurgles of the empty stomach: has anything ever been so hilarious? – *raising* a child makes you old old old. By old I mean responsible, and by responsible I mean stodgily concerned with money. Suddenly you need money for everything, none of which is Donna Karan or a day of beauty at a local spa. None of which is even, in my case, a decent pair of underpants, or a trip to the dentist to get my teeth cleaned.

You peer at the tender pink gums of your little one and try to read them as you would tea leaves: Is major orthodontia in your future? You watch him toddle across the living room, pitch a Beanie out of his crib, and find yourself wondering: Is there a God, in the form of a full-ride sports scholarship to some prestigious university?

These are the times that try women's souls, especially the soul of the enlightened woman, the good, competent woman, who chose her mate because he picked up his socks, put down the seat, could cook a decent piece of fish and wash a wool sweater without shrinking it, laughed at her jokes, appreciated the fact she could do a swan dive and he couldn't. Nice guys no longer finish last; they are snapped up by women who need a mate and not a meal ticket. Until there's a baby, who *does* need a meal ticket, not to mention someone to feed her the meal, then wipe the rest of it off the wall.

I couldn't follow the line of this reasoning much further than this. All I knew was that I suddenly had the feeling that Mary Rose had – how retro this sounds, but I can't help it – landed a big fish. Ward was in love with her, wanted this baby, made six figures a year –

Suddenly, there was a knock on the window. I leapt, shrieked, which stopped Stella crying instantly. Audra's face, dewy, recently facialed, peered in at us. She waggled her eyebrows and blinked her eyes madly at Stella. She had single-carat diamond studs in her ears, I noticed. I rolled down the window, which always stuck halfway down. I peered out over the edge of the glass, like a freedom fighter peering out of the bunker.

'We should have lunch sometime.'

'We should?'

'Let me phone you next week. We need to catch up.'

'Those are lovely earrings, Audra,' I said.

'These?' Her hands flew to her earlobes, where she twirled

the studs around as if she were adjusting the dials of a ham radio. She leaned closer. 'They're CZ,' she stage whispered. 'Don't tell Hank. He thinks he bought them for me for our fortieth. He did buy diamonds. Then I took them back and bought these instead.'

I didn't ask why she didn't want the diamonds, or what she did with the extra cash, but it brought to mind something that, I'm ashamed to say, made me feel much better. I remembered something about Ward, something I'd thought I should tell Mary Rose, then forgot about because it didn't seem terribly important, something I heard Ward say that night they'd been arguing about Ward's ex-wife out on the deck. It may have been nothing. It may have been Ward misspeaking. It may have been an honest mistake. Don't imagine it was me mis-eavesdropping; no one hears better than a new mother. When Mary Rose asked Ward how long he had been married to Lynne, he said fifteen months. It had been closer to fifteen years. I said nothing then, didn't want Mary Rose, who is so private, to know I'd been listening. I thought, Fifteen months, fifteen years, what's the difference? Anyway, it's none of my business.

Maybe Ward wasn't the Catch-of-the-Day after all. This is the uncharitable thought that perked me right up and made me tell Audra I would love to have lunch with her.

A few days later the Blazers played the Spurs, the game carried on network TV. Why a network broadcast was so important to the basketball fans of our city is unclear: Our team seemed to enjoy losing before a national audience and the sportscasters inevitably spent most of their time talking about our collective lack of self-esteem. Our feelings were always hurt. The local press would then rail for days about an East Coast bias, even though the Spurs were based in San Antonio.

Before I went to Mary Rose's for the game, I consulted the
back of Lyle's head. He had washed his hair that morning and
it smelled like mint. The basement was cold, mildewy. Itchy
Sister slept on the futon in front of the space heater. Lyle
refused to watch basketball, claimed his disinterest in professional sports made him less doltish than the average guy, said I
should be grateful he wasn't glued to the TV all weekend long.

'You're just glued to the computer.'

Tap-tap-tap, tap-tap-tap. He didn't even hear the insult. I
looked over his shoulder, white letters jerkily scrolling up the
screen. 'Rangor's ethereal shield shimmers slightly in the
setting sun.' *Yeccch.*

I bit my lips to keep myself from shrieking, 'How can you
take this stuff seriously?!' I was already five years older than
Lyle, and didn't want to sound like this mother.

'The thing is,' I said, 'I keep feeling like I should say
something to Mary Rose. It seems like no big deal, but Ward
intentionally didn't tell her about Lynne in the first place,
then he tries to minimize the marriage by making it sound as if
it was so disastrous it only lasted a little over a year. I know I
would think twice before getting involved with someone like
that. I mean, yes, I know, she's already involved, in that she's
going to have his baby, but why compound the problem?'

'Sounds like you've already got it figured out.'

'No. I don't. That's why I'm asking you.'

'God damn rock trolls,' he said to the screen. 'Let me just
cast a spell here and I'll be right with you.' Lyle stared into the
screen, tap-tap-tap.

'Knock knock.'

Tap-tap-tap.

'*Who's there?* Stepfather.'

Tap-tap-tap.

'*Stepfather who?* One step father and I'll let you have it.'

'What are you talking about?' he asked, irritated.

48

'Nothing,' I said.

When I finally got to Mary Rose's apartment the first quarter was half over, Blazers up by three. The same principles governing international air travel apply to going anywhere with an infant: You've got to be ready to leave an hour before you actually take off. When I was in a state, I forgot this. Once, ten minutes late to somewhere, I found myself wandering from room to room with Stella perched on one hip, a pink disposable diaper in one hand, a lightbulb in the other.

Mary Rose's apartment was dark, though the Mowers and Rakers truck was parked in its usual place on the street beneath the branches of the ornamental plums. Maybe Mary Rose was napping. Maybe she had popped out to the store to pick up some snacks. This was not like Mary Rose. She was organized in a way that puts those of us who wander around carrying diapers and lightbulbs to shame.

I was let in by Frick or Frack, one of Mary Rose's downstairs neighbors across the staircase from Mrs. Wanamaker. I could hear the game blaring through Mrs. Wanamaker's door, Mrs. Wanamaker clucking to Elmo, her dog, about the Blazers' disinclination to take it to the hoop.

Frick and Frack were either Tom and Bob or Greg and Ted. Mary Rose, used to working with high school boys with exotic multisyllabic names, could never remember. They wrote for the local alternative newspaper. Mary Rose always knew when they were under deadline because she'd hear the buzz of their coffee grinder at four in the morning. They volunteered to pound in lawn signs for local political campaigns, held summer solstice parties, and seemed in all ways like good neighbors. Mary Rose said they were looking to move, however, so they didn't wind up evicted when Mr. D'Addio finally unloaded the place. There was a rumor that someone had made an offer.

Mary Rose threw open her front door before I reached the

49

top of the stairs. Her raspberry V-neck sweater was stretched out at the hem as if she'd squatted and pulled it over her knees. An old trick. How to turn an ordinary cotton sweater into maternity wear.

Mary Rose was just entering her fourth month but was already beginning to show. It is a myth that you never show until your sixth month. You 'show' as early as six weeks. You show that a woman can look just like a filing cabinet.

Mary Rose held open her door, pale and silent. Normally, she oohed and cooed over Stella, calling her the Perfect Wonderment and admiring her lavender-and-white-striped all-cotton sleep sack. Instead, Mary Rose stroked Stella's fat wrist. Stella sucked her thumb and stared back at her.

'What have I done, Stella?' her voice cracked.

In the living room, scattered over the low coffee table, illuminated by a tensor lamp Mary Rose had dragged in from her night table, were dozens of photocopied articles on pregnancy, compulsively annotated in purple ink in a sinewy hand, the corners ferociously stapled a half-dozen times.

They were from Audra, who'd collected them over the years. For future reference, apparently. Mary Rose had come home this afternoon to find the padded envelope propped against the wall beside her mail slot.

'How nice of her,' I said. I couldn't think of anything else to say.

Mary Rose sat on the edge of the table, her long hands between her knees. She told me how this morning she and Fleabo, her right-hand mower, had gone to pick up some zoo doo. Our city is very proud of its zoo. Besides offering jazz concerts in the summer they also give away, by appointment only, magnificent loaves of elephant manure to anyone who'll come and haul it away. Mary Rose swore by zoo doo. It was cheap, easy on the roots of roses and radishes alike, environmentally correct. She collected a truckload of it once in the spring and once in the fall. Because Mowers and Rakers had been unusually busy since September, she hadn't yet gotten around to it.

Now, however, she was entering her fourth month of pregnancy. Now, her first thought when she opened her eyes in the morning was, When's my nap? Day in, day out, she felt like a bumbling sleeping-pill swallower whose friends were forcing her to walk circles in her living room, slapping her cheeks and pouring black coffee down her throat. She raked with the wrong side of the rake, put the milk in the cupboard and the Cheerios in the fridge, mailed bills with no stamps.

Mary Rose had wanted to skip the zoo doo, but Fleabo, dedicated to saving the planet, insisted. Fleabo was Michael Fleabowski, a twenty-nine-year-old Zen Buddhist. She had stolen him from our city's most popular nursery, where he had been in charge of shrubs. He was a familiar type in our city. An avid recycler, a student of yoga, Fleabo wore his lustrous bark-brown hair in a thick braid.

He was adamant about the zoo doo. If they didn't fertilize now they would be forced to use some fast-acting chemical stuff in the spring. He promised to drive, shovel, and buy Mary Rose a smoothie when they were done.

Mel, the retired volunteer in charge of zoo doo, let them in the zoo service entrance at 7:00 A.M. The elephant biscuits were piled at the far end of the elephant pen. As you approached you could see them steaming in the cold morning air, mounds of olive-green hassocks studded with bits of straw. Interested in all matters digestive these days, I was naturally fascinated hearing about this.

Mel operated the bright yellow front-loader, scooping and dumping several hundred pounds of manure into the bed of Fleabo's pick-up.

'I was standing next to the truck and just as Mel was about to let loose I saw my Swiss clippers, that really good pair I hadn't been able to find for months? They were lying in the back of the truck. I didn't think. I saw them and I reached for them and there I am, suddenly, up to my armpit in it. Do you think I'll get toxoplasmosis?'

A disease that can cause blindness, fetal brain damage, and malformation of the head in unborn children. 'Isn't that from eating raw meat and cleaning the cat litter box?' I asked.

'But if you can get it from tiny cat turds . . .'

'It's not the same thing,' I said. 'It's a parasite thing.'

'Zoo doo probably causes something worse. They just haven't discovered it yet.'

'Do yourself a favor. Don't read this stuff.'

'I already have. Twice. It's important to know these things.'

According to the articles, all culled from respectable newspapers and medical journals, Mary Rose had done nearly everything humanly possible outside mainlining powerful recreational drugs to ensure her He-bean would be deformed and brain damaged. Brain damaged and deformed, words no mother-to-be ever utters aloud but thinks about from morning till night.

Mary Rose had had two glasses of red wine before she knew she was pregnant.

She had been stuck in a number of traffic jams, which increased her exposure to carbon monoxide.

Ate on several occasions what she presumed, based on other articles she had read, was a high-protein, low-fat, highly nourishing meal of white fish, thereby exposing herself to pesticides and mercury.

Visited a mutual friend in his darkroom (photographic chemicals; general deformation).

Burned rubber on a few occasions in the Mowers and Rakers truck (cadmium from the tires; retards growth).

Snitched a squirt of someone's spray deodorant from the medicine cabinet in the Barons' bathroom on Thanksgiving (aerosol spray; miscarriage).

Got stuck a few times in the smoking section of a restaurant (self-explanatory).

Had a few smokes herself, before quitting once and for all.

Just the day before, feeling a cold coming on, she had taken a hot bath, which can cause fetal brain damage, and an aspirin, which can cause miscarriage. She had taken nose drops, which contract the blood vessels in the nose as well as the placenta, thereby reducing the flow of oxygen to the fetus.

'I drank *tap* water. I've been drinking tap water since day one. Eight glasses a day of lead and industrial toxins. No one told me I was supposed to drink bottled water. What am I supposed to do now?'

'Cut out booze, stay away from paint fumes, and stay away from all this crap.' I laid Stella between us on the nubby brown couch and began stuffing the articles back in the padded envelope.

'What if I'm carrying a monster?'

'You're not carrying a monster.'

'No one knows that for a fact.'

'Mary Rose, no one knows anything for a fact. Haven't you figured that out yet? These scientists writing all this don't know what's going on. They get grants and come up with these wacko statistics just so they'll get more grants to study the thing further. All it succeeds in doing in scaring the bejesus out of us. Pregnancies continue on their merry way, just as they always have. Here's the toxoplasmosis thing – one to three births in four thousand.'

'But somebody has to be the one to three.' Mary Rose stood in the middle of her small, dark living room cracking her knuckles. A few strands of her dark blond hair had escaped from her bun and hung down her back.

'Mary Rose. You absolutely cannot worry. I'm not saying this just because I don't like to see you all worked up. It's not good for the baby. Stress in the mother during pregnancy can cause the baby to be anxious and fussy.'

'Oh, great, there's nothing worse than a two-headed baby with colic.'

'Try to relax.'

'So you're saying if the hot tubs and the tap water and the exhaust fumes won't get me, worrying about the hot tubs and the tap water and the exhaust fumes will.'

'Nothing will get you.'

I sat her down on the sofa, went into the kitchen, and made her some cinnamon toast. When I brought it back, she had Stella nestled in her lap, absentmindedly stroking her black hair while she watched the game.

I could not bring myself to tell her about Ward.

I had known Mary Rose at that time for exactly eight years. I remember because it was just after Christmas when I came up from Los Angeles to begin production on *Romeo's Dagger.* I knew her well enough to know this fretting and cuticle-chewing was not like her. Mary Rose had her own business, don't forget, her .25 ACP, her time-share and financial instruments. She was the most level-headed woman I knew, level-headed and self-sufficient. Poor her.

Normally Mary Rose went home to La Mirada, California, to celebrate Christmas with her father, Roy, but she thought boarding an airplane was surely courting disaster. What if the cabin suddenly lost pressure and the oxygen mask didn't come down? What if the person sitting next to her had been exposed to German measles?

She wound up spending the day at the Barons'. To her great embarrassment, she received more presents than anyone else. A green maternity top with matching leggings from Audra prompted Little Hank to call her the Jolly Green Giant. Ha-ha! From Audra she also received an antique rocking chair and footstool for nursing. Ward gave Mary Rose a sapphire ring to match her eyes, which were dark brown. She put it on for the evening, then couldn't get it off. The silver punch bowl brimming with non-fat egg-substitute nog prompted Mary Rose to stop for a milkshake on her way home.

I was wrapped up in test-driving some traditions with which to burden Stella, featuring an expensive felt Advent calendar, monogrammed stockings, midnight mass, and sing-along *Messiah* at a downtown concert hall.

Lyle participated – it was Christmas, after all – but begrudgingly. He said Stella was too young to remember any of this, and why was I exhausting myself even further. All Stella needed, he claimed, was a single present to open, so that she might have the pleasure of ripping the used wrapping paper and gumming the ribbon.

He turned out to be right, but what of it?

4

You've probably figured out that things could be better between me and Lyle. Sometimes, when I'm walking Stella up and down our tiny living room, lifting my knees as high as an overachieving majorette, because that's how Stella likes it, I wonder why I gave up Los Angeles for a life in this soggy burg with a man five years my junior who turns a cold shoulder to his daughter, preferring to wage war with monsters on-line, and poorly imaged monsters at that.

I don't wonder too much, because all roads always lead to the existence of Stella. If I hadn't had him, I wouldn't have her.

Lyle was not always insensitive; or else he kept his insensitive tendencies hidden until the time came when he no longer cared what I thought. He no longer cared what I thought around the time Stella joined our household, when, to tell the truth, I no longer cared what he thought, by which I mean there were days when the voluptuous round of nursing Stella, changing her diaper, bathing her, cuddling her, walking her, prevented me from ever getting out of my bathrobe, which Lyle interpreted as an act of hostility directed against himself. Once he said it was like I was having an affair. I acted shocked. Of course, he was right.

This is an old story: how a couple goes from quaking love to sluggish indifference.

Lyle and I met at a film seminar hosted by the media bigwigs of our city. It was a gala event, or so I was told when they invited me to come and speak. The other guests were writers, directors, and producers who were famous to aspiring writers, directors, and producers. The seminar was apparently not prestigious enough to attract writers, directors, and producers famous to the movie-going public at large.

Still, it was nice. It was April, a time in our city when the rhododendrons explode and the weather skids from bright sun to thundering hail in minutes. Double rainbows arch over Mt. Hood.

Romeo's Dagger had just finished principal photography. I spoke to a crowd of three hundred and fifty on the difficulties of making the independent feature, showed a reel of dailies, answered questions, left out the part about the role of pure, glorious, sad, simple luck. I wanted the seminar people to feel I was worth what they were paying me.

Between sessions there was scheduled forty-five minutes of schmoozing over coffee and cookies in the foyer. This gave the aspirants who had paid a considerable amount to attend the seminar a chance to hound the participants into reading their screenplays. I had three tucked under my arm when Lyle approached me.

He had nothing in his hands besides a paper water cup chewed around the rim. I engaged him in conversation the better to exclude the aspirants of prey who may have wanted a favor. I stood closer to him than was absolutely necessary. He wore a yellow button-down shirt that smelled fresh from the wash.

Here is a tip: If ever you go to one of these things and feel too shy to approach the keynote speaker during the event itself, just wait. After the coffee and cookies are cleared from the foyer and the microphone is disconnected and the lectern shunted to the wings, the special guest turns instantly into a nobody at loose ends in an unfamiliar city, with nothing but the prospect of a room-service dinner and a night of cable TV ahead of her.

Unless, of course, a Lyle approaches you. My hotel was eight or so blocks away, not too far to walk on a melon-colored evening in early spring. Lyle's car was parked in the same direction. We walked, bumping shoulders. I was aware of behaving in a very friendly manner, more so than I might have normally. He struck me as very green. Youngish, if not young. I took him seriously only in that by making it appear as if I knew him better than I did, the people at the seminar whom I did take seriously – a director I thought I might one day work with, for example – would see that I had something to do, that I was not alone in this city. How embarrassing it would have been. Me, alone, here. Of all places. For don't forget, *Romeo's Dagger* was shot here, the exteriors anyway. By all rights I should have been surrounded by local people who had worked on the production. I don't know where they all were. They had gone back to Los Angeles, or did not care to cough up the price of the seminar. Maybe it was the fine weather. Maybe there was a basketball game.

The Barons should have been there, Dicky and Audra at least. But Dicky was in New York, doing something infomercial-related. He had left a message at my hotel along with a funereal floral arrangement starring a dozen salmon-orange gladioli.

Audra was still miffed. She had not been hundred percent pleased with the actress cast to play her. Actually, she had been pleased at first. Then came a story in the local paper. A reporter had spent a day on the set. The story appeared on the front page of the Living Arts section, with a picture of the actress playing Audra and a drop quote beneath it saying she had captured perfectly 'a woman of a certain age frantically clutching at the last strands of youth.'

Lyle had a navy-blue nylon knapsack from which he took a small brown notebook, a cheap pen that you might pick up at one of those old-fashioned kinds of businesses, a shoe-repair shop perhaps, threaded through the spiral. He kept stopping and writing down things I said. Things not worth remembering, clichéd observations about movie-making that I hadn't myself experienced but had gotten from a book on Francis Coppola.

I was flattered that I was so quotable, but it was that cheap blue-and-white plastic pen. It was like a homely kitten rescued from the pound. He was left-handed, and wrote with the notebook propped against his thigh, his hand curved, crablike.

He invited me to his loft. A man with a loft – is there anything sexier than that? There, I saw the huge Hawaiian Punch murals. I knew nothing about art, but I saw that he had framed his smaller canvases and had then painted over the frame, as if it wasn't even there. I pronounced this witty and brilliant, not knowing he had snatched the idea from a local street poet, also a self-described artist, known mostly for a poem in which he compares an overgrown zucchini to his own penis.

When we made love that night in my hotel room – they put me up in the same place where the NBA put their teams when they came here to play – in his ferocious passion he kept bonking what I took to be one of my ovaries with his hip bone. Maybe it was not an ovary, but considering all that would happen to us I like the metaphor. My bed was large as an ocean-going raft, and part of the thrill of being with Lyle was wondering whether Michael Jordan had ever had this room. The thrill for me, anyway.

The thrill for Lyle, I suppose, was that I was a producer from Los Angeles. I wore a black linen jacket, thigh-length, jeans, and a bright white T-shirt. My chic producer's costume, created for me by an assistant who had told me, no offense, that I dressed like an aging sorority girl and how did I expect to get anything going, looking like that?

Lyle was at that time considering switching from being a would-be painter to being a would-be guy-having-something-to-do-with-film. (Later, he decided that he wanted to be a would-be-guy-having-something-to-do-with-the-Web,   but while in the research stage, discovered Realm of the Elf, which is where we find him today.)

Like me, Lyle had no special talent but had stumbled upon a handy situation. In his case it was a modest settlement from a law suit. He had accidentally driven off a low cliff while three-wheeling in Colorado, and his lawyer had squeezed sixty thousand dollars from the Japanese company that made the three-wheeler, citing a failure to notify the consumer that driving a three-wheeler over a low cliff could be hazardous. Lyle had broken his arm in three places, then leased the loft.

I knew nothing then about Lyle's accident and settlement. All I saw were his lowriding faded jeans, the upper thighs stained with swipes of paint where he had obviously wiped his hands in a distracted moment. An artist. Sigh. The occupation is to our generation what soldiering was to a previous one. The romance lasted three perfect days. We rented a bicycle built for two, ate double-scoop ice cream cones in a downpour, and did just about everything else you can think of that appears in a montage of two people falling in love. He failed to mention that he was also a photocopier repairman. Not that it would have mattered.

It helped that I lived at the bottom of the country and he lived at the top. Being apart fed flames that may have otherwise petered out in a matter of weeks. There's no telling, of course. Only after we were married did he tell me about the settlement. By then, the money had run out. I found myself married not to a successful painter but to a photocopier repairman, owner of Itchy Sister, the ancient, tumor-filled

Rhodesian Ridgeback with chronic allergies and huge vet bills. He found himself married not to an independent film producer in a black linen blazer but to a pregnant woman.

I discovered my condition five weeks after the wedding. In a heated moment he accused me of using him as a sperm donor, to which I replied that there may be a shortage of many things in this world, but sperm was not one of them.

When I was able to pry Lyle from the computer, he made a lot of noise about how we should go out more, just like the old days.

'You mean before Stella,' I always said, hurt.

One thing Lyle and I agreed on was Chinese food. We shared a passion for limp greasy 'American' Chinese food – chow mein, chop suey, and egg foo young – and indulged as often as we were speaking, knowing that soon Stella would be of an age when we would be forced to order more respectable dishes in the interest of setting a good example. Or at least I knew this. Who knows what Lyle thought.

Judy's Ho-Wa, our favorite restaurant, was in Chinatown. In our city this consists of three blocks of Chinese restaurants and one shop that sells cheap vases, plastic chopsticks, and still, as advertised in the window, GENUINE MT. ST. HELEN ASS.

One night, when Lyle was feeling less defensive than usual and, to be fair, I was feeling more talkative and less resentful than usual, I teased him, which he liked. Watching Lyle try to slurp down beef chow mein without splattering any on his pristine white Oxford button-down or blue silk tie was endlessly amusing. His overdeveloped sense of order forbade him from removing his tie or tucking one of the stained red cloth napkins into his collar. He would thrust his chin out over his plate, pinch a few gray noodles between the plastic chopsticks, then slowly lift them straight from the plate to his mouth. It was like watching a crane at work on a construction site.

'Why not just live for the moment and stick that napkin under your chin?' I asked. 'No one's watching.'

'I wouldn't be here in a shirt and tie if I didn't live for the moment.'

'I do have one of Stella's bibs in my purse,' I said.

'Is it the one with the green hippos on it?'

'I think so.'

'I was hoping it was the one that says "Princess of Wails." That one I like.'

We could banter like this for hours, which was a useful technique for avoiding discussing our problems, which . . . hey! when we nattered on like this, we didn't have any problems! It was like being so exhausted you didn't have the energy to know you were exhausted. We were laughing, we were chatting, so what was the problem?

Suddenly, at the back of the restaurant, at a huge round table, the kind only Chinese restaurants seem to specialize in, I saw Dicky Baron. He was wearing the same heavy, blue plaid flannel shirt he'd worn on Thanksgiving, the same baggy exercise pants with the stripe up the side. I knew that outfit: It was the outfit of the person who had gained weight and didn't fit comfortably in anything else he owned, but didn't want to buy any new clothes because that would mean accepting the bigger body.

I knew this because I was also this person. I'm referring, of course, to the toll of motherhood. I imagine you're a few sentences ahead of me here, thinking I'll reveal interesting if vaguely repellent tales of stretch marks, swinging breasts, and snaking varicosities that strike everywhere you can imagine, not just behind the knees.

You're thinking maybe I'll bemoan the fact that never again will I stroll down the beach in my thong bikini. The truth is, even in my most nubile days, I never strolled anywhere in a bikini; I lay on one side, flipped hurriedly to the other, then rushed headlong into the ocean, hoping my behavior would be misinterpreted as reckless abandon and not a desire to take advantage of the world's largest bathing suit cover-up.

But giving birth causes things to stretch, sag, droop, and dangle a lot less than you may imagine. What happens, mainly, is that your top priority ceases to be maintaining that little indentation on either side of your tush. You don't care. You have become an anarchist of the flesh, a truly dangerous woman.

Until, of course, the day you begin worrying that your child will be ostracized at nursery school because her mommy is a tubola. Then it's back to carrot sticks and sit-ups; the world once more safe for democracy. I am not there yet. I asked Lyle to pass the spring rolls, please.

Dicky was with a party of a dozen or so, deep into solving the only story problem from high school math that ever rears its head in real life: ciphering who owes what from a single, scribbled ticket. Our booth was near the cash register; Dicky would have to lumber our way.

There was still time. I hissed, 'Lyle, don't turn around, do *not* turn around. There's Dicky Baron. Switch places with me.'

'What?'

'Switch places with me! He won't recognize you – oh, hi, Dicky.'

'Hey, hey, hey! It's my producer! Dot, Martin, come meet my producer!' Dicky plunked into the booth next to me, snatching a piece of spring roll from my plate and lobbing it into his mouth. His breath smelled like whiskey and, beneath that, something sour. 'Brooke, you look as if you've lost, what, twelve to thirteen pounds since Thanksgiving? And you're still breast-feeding right? You look great for a woman who's still breast-feeding.'

Dot and Martin, who seemed anxious to get on with things, nevertheless allowed themselves to be introduced. Dot was a former Olympic silver medalist who now sold toilet paper to large institutions; Martin was a South African gynecologist who enjoyed months of airplay for having gone to prison for inseminating infertility patients with sperm from the same donor: his own father.

This took longer for Dicky to explain than I have here, but Dicky, as I've said, had a tendency to go on and on, and why duplicate his conversation here? Dot and Martin cracked open their fortune cookies, read their fortunes, then traded and read the other's, before the slot in Dicky's monologue appeared in which they could mutter 'Nice to meet you' and be on their way.

'Those are what I call colorful careers,' said Lyle after Dot and Martin had left.

'No more colorful than mine or anybody else's in FF. Are you done with that other spring roll?'

FF stood for Formerly Famous, the informal support group that Dicky belonged to, composed of people who had all managed to grab the gold ring of fame and had either dropped it or had it wrenched from their hands by the world's need for new celebrity.

'What do you do?' I said. 'All sit around and complain about not being invited to be on *The New Hollywood Squares*?'

'Do they even still have *The New Hollywood Squares*?' asked Lyle.

'Did they ever have *The New Hollywood Squares*?' I said. 'Maybe we made it up.'

'Formerly Famous is a support group,' said Dicky, irritated. 'We're trying to get our lives back together. I really feel for a lot of them, you know? They have no options. I'm in a little better position. I'm not just anybody. R— played me in a movie. I've got a track record. I've had a movie made. Brooke, I'm sure it's the same with you – even though you're doing the mom thing, you still get calls. It's harder to get *out* of the business than get *into* it. 'Who do I sleep with to get *off* this picture?' Remember when you used to say that on the set? Brooke? You were hilarious before you had a kid. I guess motherhood kind of takes the sheen off the brain or something, huh? Anyway, I've got a few things I'm pitching around, a few things. Brooke, you might be interested in this one: revisiting the people of *Romeo's Dagger* ten years later. It could be called *As I Lay Down the Dagger*. I think there could be real interest in that, in what happened to me since Jen's death. It's a truly American story, a story for the zeros, don't you think? I tried to called *Oprah*. Remember, Brooke, when I did *Oprah*? You know, to give her production company first shot at it. It's just common courtesy. Or maybe it would be better to write the book of ten years later, and have Oprah feature it in her book club. What do you think?'

I concentrated on chasing a few soy-soaked bean sprouts around my plate. Lyle listened. He sat forward, nodding his head, folding and unfolding the thin paper sleeve from his chopsticks. 'Could be interesting, Dick, could be. What *have* you been doing the last ten years?'

'Living at home,' said Dicky.

'Well, just off the top of my head, I think you might need more of a plot. But that's Brooke's department.' Lyle nudged my toe with his beneath the table, a prompt that I should be participating in this ridiculous conversation. I ignored him, ate my sprouts.

'But how does it appeal to you as a guy?' said Dicky. 'I mean, does it speak to you? It'll be the new *Clerks*, remember *Clerks*? The movie about the two losers who work in a convenience store? It'll be like, see how women are taking over the planet? Women are taking over, forcing guys like me – guys who would be winning World War II if it wasn't for all these ball busters out there – to mooch off his parents.'

*   *   *

In the Volvo, driving to pick up Stella at the baby-sitter's (a single mother and assistant D.A. who lived two doors down, and whose 18-month-old son I would watch on occasion), Lyle said, 'Dicky's kind of an interesting character, huh?'

It was raining hard; in the headlights it looked as if nickels were falling from the sky. The windshield wipers madly *whopp-whopp-whopped*. My stomach hurt, indigestion. I was irritated, then irritated at my irritation, an emotional Escher. This was Lyle's finest quality: giving other human beings the benefit of the doubt. He was kind! He was tolerant! He was all those other things that appear in the hokey prayers of kitchen samplers the world over. Still, he should have more sense.

'Emphasis on the word *character*,' I said. I thought I was being good, leaving it at that.

'Yeah, he's a bit odd, but he may really have something there,' said Lyle.

'Uh-huh,' I said.

'I mean, a movie about a guy stuck living home. It sounds boring, but it could be kind of cool.'

This was more than I could stand. 'Are you out of your mind? *As I Lay Down the Dagger?*'

'It has nice Faulknerian ring to it.'

'*Faulknerian ring!* FAULKNERIAN RING!' I was panting. 'And what was all that crap about how he'd be fighting in World War II if women weren't ball busters? Don't you see anything wrong with that logic? Dicky is an insufferable idiot. Dicky has always been an insufferable idiot. Two hours of Dicky sitting at home being an insufferable idiot is not a movie.'

Lyle took his eyes off the road. 'Maybe you should think about getting back to work.'

'What does that have to do with anything?'

'This seems to have struck a nerve.'

'No, Lyle, you've struck a nerve. How can you think Dicky

is interesting? He's about as interesting as those morons you play with on-line.'

Lyle pursed his lips, said nothing. I could tell I'd hurt his feelings. Well, so what? I wrapped my arms around myself. I couldn't wait to get my arms around Stella, to bury my nose in the folds of her neck. Stella, I could talk to. She was easily the wisest person in this family. She would never marry someone like her father.

5

It was drizzling when I arrived at the Barons' for lunch, the clouds so low it felt as if I could reach up and bury my hand in one. It was the day after Lyle and I had run into Dicky. Audra had called me that morning and asked me for that day. At first I thought it was odd, this sudden urgency, but I was always happy to have an outing for Stella in the afternoon, especially now that the weather had gotten dreary, so I went. I suppose that is just an excuse.

The house was situated so that you weren't sure which was the proper door to knock on. Either way you felt ridiculous. The front door, the proper door for someone who had been there as infrequently as I had, was around the back, facing the city and the wooded slope where Ward and Mary Rose had frolicked and fallen in love. The back door was right off the carport, but had no number on it and looked suited only for family and service people.

I extricated Stella from her seat, hoisted her diaper bag onto my shoulder, and slogged through the wet grass to the front door. I knocked until my knuckles hurt. No one answered.

I then slogged back to the back door. My flats were soaked. No answer there, either. I wondered if maybe Audra hadn't asked me for today after all, then I heard someone cry, 'Damn you!'

It came from behind the garage. I minced down the gravel drive, my feet freezing in my cheap wet shoes. I had unearthed the black leather flats from beneath a jumble of hightop cross-trainers and a pair of brown leather work Oxfords with lug soles. The Oxfords are the type that look stunning on twenty-year-old waifs with thin ankles and no responsibilities, but made me look like a Russian street sweeper.

I found Audra kneeling on the patio, which was tiled with imported Spanish pavers.

She was stricken, staring down at a pile of brown twigs as if it was a beloved pet that had been clipped by a passing car and lay whimpering and panting in its final moments of life. The twigs had apparently been pulled from a hole beside the pergola that spanned the back of the garage, the only place on the property that got enough sun for such an intrepid horticultural enterprise as *Paraiso Mexicano*.

She stood up, bits of moss clinging to the knees of her cashmere pants. 'My bougainvillea,' she said. 'It didn't look very firmly anchored and so I was just trying to pat it . . .' The twigs were in fact the roots, parts of which were blackened with rot.

'Maybe you should try some wisteria. That's supposed to be hardy.'

'Oh!' She flung the dead plant onto the stucco bench. 'I just hate all those frilly plants. Big Hank was right. As usual. Money can't buy a micro-climate. It's cold out here.' She pulled her sweater across her middle and reached for Stella. 'Come to Aunt Audra, you precious person. Well, I'm off to PV on Thursday anyway. I'll get plenty of bougainvillea there.'

'PV?'

'Puerto Vallarta. I've gone every January since before Dicky was born. I call it my month of madness!'

Audra served leftover take-out spinach fettucini. We ate off dessert plates in the formal dining room, stiff paper towels for napkins. Audra clearly hadn't given this lunch much thought. She sat sideways in her chair with her legs crossed, watching me eat.

'I need to ask a favor of you,' said Audra.

'Okay.' I cut a noodle into half-inch bits and fed a few to Stella. Her eyebrows leapt up and her little red-lipped mouth went O. I laughed. The shock of the new, her first fettucini. Audra, who I thought would have also been delighted, waited, twisting her rings.

'I'm worried about Dicky. He said he ran into you after his meeting last night. I was just wondering, are you going back to work soon, and if you are, do you have anything for Dicky to do? Or is anyone else you know in need of someone like Dicky?'

Someone like Dicky. There was no one like Dicky. Thank God in His infinite mercy. 'Well, what would he like to do?'

'That's just it. I don't think he knows. But since the movie, well, he's never been able to land anywhere, you know? And it's been how long? He's getting a little peculiar. *Entre nous*, he can't bear to look at the Sunday *Times* anymore. He can't even be in the same room with it. Especially the Arts & Leisure section.'

'What's wrong with the Arts & Leisure section?'

'He says it reminds him that he's a nobody. He had me call our local *Times* distributor and see if I couldn't get someone to remove the section before the paper is delivered. Now he wants the Book Review taken out too – says it reminds him of all the books being made into movies. This isn't normal, is it?'

She sniffed, dabbed at her eyes with the tips of her fingers.

I dug in Stella's bag for a jar of carrots so Audra wouldn't see me see her cry. Is this what happened to children eventually? They grew up and got weird, and your no-win position was either to try and relieve their distress without really helping them, or tell them to get over it, thereby causing further anguish. This was probably part of the reason Audra was desperate for a grandchild. You got to love them when they were still perfect like Stella, and if you were lucky you'd be dead by the time they grew up and eloped with someone with a prison record.

Audra asked how many ear infections Stella had had. What was her eyesight like? How many diapers did she have a day? And did I give her fluoride? And wasn't it difficult to clip her nails? They were so tiny. And was I simply suffocating with love for her?

I said, 'You of all people should know how it is. You've had three.'

'Believe me, you forget.'

'I thought that was labor and delivery.'

Audra tried to smile, but her orange lipsticked lips kept crumpling.

'I could try to make a few phone calls, for Dicky, I mean, to see if anyone needs someone on the set or something. Other than that, I'm not sure . . .'

'Oh, Dicky is the least of my worries.'

Wait, wasn't Dicky the one she was really worried about? Wasn't that why I was here?'

'Ward . . .' She started to cry in earnest. Stella stopped eating and stared. Oh no. All I could think was that Ward was sick. He was HIV positive, had leukemia, something.

'What's wrong with Ward?'

'Oh, nothing. I mean nothing terrible. Well, actually, it's awful. Lynne won't give him a divorce.'

'Whoa. I thought they were divorced. I know Mary Rose thinks they're divorced.'

'Ward is my favorite child. I expect this to go no further than this table. Ward is my favorite child. But he has no sense of the consequences of his actions. He's feckless. They started divorce proceedings when he was dating someone else, then they – Ward and I think her name was . . . could it have been Bryn? – broke up and he lost interest. In proceeding with the divorce, I mean. Mary Rose is like a daughter to us. This will crush her, I expect. It will ruin her life. Ward, despite his lack of follow-through, is still quite a catch.'

I wiped Stella's mouth with the corner of my paper towel napkin: a mistake. It left a faint red dash beneath her lip, and her face folded into the warm-up for a shriek. I admit: In a moment of self-pity I'd thought this too, that Ward would be a guy worth having around. Now I bristled. Here Audra was weeping because Ward was such an irresponsible lout, then saying that he was still a 'catch' – suddenly I hated that whole concept, too – and that Mary Rose would be ruined, *ruined!* – when she found out.

Mary Rose was made of tougher stuff than that. Indeed, as if to prove it to myself, I called her from the car to see if I might stop by. I said I had a *Sports Illustrated* article on the Blazers to give her. My excuse, although considering what I had to tell her, I don't think I really needed one.

When I got there she was standing in front of the hallway mirror in a periwinkle-and-green-striped tank suit. The vertical stripes became paler as the fabric stretched thin over her abdomen. Dr. Vertamini had suggested Mary Rose take a prenatal water aerobics class in order to stay in shape during her pregnancy. I had pointed out that staying in shape made labor and delivery easier, as do pennies found beneath sofa cushions help pay the mortgage.

'You know me, a dedicated penny pincher.' Then she struck a Virgin Mary pose, hands folded discreetly over her belly. 'I felt the He-bean move. Three days ago. Me and Fleabo were raking leaves and suddenly it was like somebody opened a bottle of champagne in there. That's it, isn't it?'

She told me how it went: Fleabo got one look at her face,

dropped his rake, and urged her to sit down. When she assured him that she was fine, he rushed into the house and returned with a glass of water, that universal non-remedy that gives those untrained in first aid an opportunity to leave the side of the stricken without appearing cowardly.

Mary-Rose was too shy to tell Fleabo it was only the first stirrings of the He-bean. No reason to worry; reason, in fact, to rejoice. She was only fifteen weeks along. According to one of her articles, fetal movement was rarely felt until week twenty in a first pregnancy, conventional medical wisdom assuming that a woman who had never before been pregnant might mistake this startling effervescence for the humdrum gurgling of indigestion. But Mary Rose was not mistaken. She recognized the He-bean's flailings instantly. Her spirits made the space shuttle look like one of those Wilbur and Orville Wright contraptions that only made it four feet off the ground.

The He-bean squirms! The He-bean lives! He was alive and healthy, a prodigy of gestation.

And Mary Rose, proud of having felt the champagne bubbles earlier than most, came to see herself as a prodigy of motherhood. Her insomnia ceased. She slept ten long, dreamless hours a night, awakened only briefly at 3:00 A.M. by the coffee grinder of Frick and Frack.

'They're moving out, did I tell you? Mr. D'Addio sold the place, finally. Frick found a fixer-upper on Pettygrove Street and Frack is putting the money down. Or the other way around. Gorgeous fig trees out front.'

'I've got some news that I don't think you're going to like to hear. But someone's got to tell you, and tell you soon. Ward is still legally married to Lynne the dog lady.'

Mary Rose rolled her lips inside her mouth, tucked her hair behind her ears, but otherwise didn't respond. 'You mean he doesn't have a decree,' she said finally.

'I mean, from what I understand, the papers were filed, and

then no one followed through. Before Ward met you there was apparently no real urgency.'

'How'd you get wind of this?'

I told her about my lunch with Audra.

'You know what frustrates me? We're talking about life in general here. You try to be optimistic, but then your worst suspicions – the ones you tried to chase from your head because you were sure you were being a pessimist – turn out to have been right all along.'

That was all she said.

Until this:

Three days later Mary Rose picked Ward up from the airport. He was returning from a shoot, a kind-to-your-dental-work chewing-gum spot in Florida. According to what Audra would later tell me, he was surprised to see her. Lynne and Bryn and all the others whose names did not rhyme apparently liked to appear independent, the better to entice her son. They made him take a cab.

As Ward waded through the crowd, garment bag slung over his bony shoulder, his thoughts fastened on the phrase 'carrying my child,' which he associated with hotel porters and Sherpas. It was fitting, then, that Mary Rose should be there.

Mary Rose looked younger than he remembered. It was her shiny dark blond hair, which she wore long around her shoulders. Her skin, which shone like old pearls, the famous glow of pregnancy. Or her clothes, which at first Ward mistook for a parochial school uniform. She wore a navy-blue suit, white dress shirt, a blue knit tie, a cap.

Only when he saw the hand-lettered sign *Mr. Barren*, did Ward realize this was some sort of practical joke. She had come to pick him up dressed up as, what? A chauffeur?

Ward tended his reputation carefully. He never allowed anyone to throw him a surprise party, never played charades or sang the national anthem at ball games. He eschewed silly hats. That anyone who knew him would subject him to this sort of dumb prank was bad enough. That Mary Rose would do this . . .

Ward worked hard at feminism, as befit a hip director of high-profile television commercials. He had convinced his peers and family that he believed women were more than creatures born to enliven cocktail parties and buy Christmas presents on his behalf. But a pregnant woman. That was something else. She was womanhood off the charts, a fever too hot to register. The Barons weren't Catholic, but Ward, during a particularly impressionable junior year abroad, had absorbed Botticelli to a dangerous degree. He had come to believe that pregnancy mysteriously and automatically conferred upon Woman a virginal grace and piety.

Yet here was Mary Rose. The woman carrying his child. Standing before him in a polyester chauffeur suit, her belly jutting out round over her waistband. She was grinning with her large lovely teeth and flapping her homemade sign.

Like many of the hip, he disapproved of many things. This, at the moment, being number one on the list.

His knot of anxiety tightened further when they reached his houseboat. After helping haul his luggage down the gangplank Mary Rose fired up his potbellied stove and kicked off her shoes, settling in. 'Ward, I really really missed you,' she said.

'Not as much as I missed you.' His usual response. 'I missed you, too' sounded rote, not creative enough for a Clio-winning director who prided himself on knowing how to talk to women.

'While you were gone I realized how much I love you. I do want to get married. I've decided.'

'I love you, too.' Rote, but impossible to improve on.

'Soon,' she said. 'We can fly to Reno. Let's go now.'

The stove, an antique, sat between the large front room, with its Adirondack furniture and plate-glass windows overlooking the river, and the small kitchen. Ward stood poised in front of the black refrigerator, a glass of club soda for Mary Rose in one hand, a goblet of red wine for himself in the other.

'We can't go to Reno. I just got off an airplane.'

'What better time? You're already packed.'

'We can't go now, just like that. What about Audra and Big Hank? It would kill them, eloping. I'm not a traditionalist, you know that, but I can't just, well, anyway, I'd like to meet your father. We'll begin planning.'

'All right,' she said. 'How about Valentine's Day?'

'Valentine's Day. That would be great.'

'We can get the license tomorrow.'

'Not two weeks from now you don't mean?'

'Valentine's Day. Yes.'

'I thought you meant a year from now. It takes time to plan a wedding.'

'You would know.'

Ward felt his intestines shift. His scrotum huddled close to his body. Batten down the hatches. He prepared himself for the onslaught of feminine fury. At last, Mary Rose *knew*. He had been bad and now she would get mad. It was axiomatic. It had happened dozens of times before. He was glad he had not handed Mary Rose the glass. Once, before, he had done something wrong and had spent the rest of the evening picking shards of crystal from his eyebrows.

'No wonder your parents weren't pressuring us to get married. I just wrote it off to their being rich liberals.'

'I really wish you wouldn't do this. It's a really sucky habit you have, baiting me all the time. If you wanted to know about my past, you should have just asked me.'

'I keep asking and asking, Ward. I didn't think to ask if you had an ex-wife until you let that one slip. Now it turns out she's not technically your ex-wife. What should I be asking? Do you have any other wives? Any other children? A season spent with Up with People!? What, Ward? What else is going on with you that I'm supposed to be asking about?'

'It's not fair. You set me up,' said Ward. 'I'm trying my best. You don't know Lynne.'

'Life is a cabaret, old chum.' Mary Rose folded her arms, tucking them into the slot between breasts and belly. She stared at him and waited.

'I haven't seen her for five years. We're married in name only. That's why I didn't tell you before. It's just a legal thing. Not even legal. Clerical.'

'I know, I know. She's in northern California at Seeing Eye Dog School.'

'She's not interested in men,' said Ward.

'She's a lesbian?'

'She likes Labrador retrievers.'

'Who can blame her?'

'There is nothing with Lynne, nothing. It's like this house-boat. I love this houseboat. I live here. It's my home, but the bank holds the mortgage.'

'What are you talking about?'

'Lynne holds the mortgage, Mary Rose. Lynne holds the mortgage, but I live in you. You're my house, my home.' He put the glasses of club soda and wine out of sight in the sink in case Mary Rose got any ideas, and knelt before her on the unfinished wood floor, laying both hands on her belly.

'Sorry, no room in the inn,' she said.

'Please,' he said.

'All that about how ridiculous it would be to rush into marriage. The only thing you were worried about rushing into was bigamy.'

'You're entitled to think less of me. Just don't cut me out of your life. Please.' His voice became a smoker's whisper. He laid his head in what was left of her lap.

'I hardly think less of you. I am impressed is what I am. I

thought men these days didn't want to commit. A wife and a girlfriend. Busy, busy.'

'So you understand?'

'Why risk endangering the baby? Stress causes the fetal lungs to mature at a faster rate. It can make the baby anxious and colicky. I'm not pissed. I am, however, going to go home and watch the rest of the Blazers-Suns game.'

She nudged his head off her thighs and struggled to her feet. She went home. Evidence, in Ward's mind, that something was wrong with her. Barring a medical emergency, no woman who boarded the houseboat at night ever left until morning. That Mary Rose left in order to watch a basketball game . . .

This was not a ploy on Mary Rose's part. Not reverse psychology or any of that. After I told her that Ward was still married, Mary Rose had responded in a more typical fashion. She was silent with hurt, then took it out on Mrs. Camanetti's holly bush. She oiled up her chain saw and took the twelve-foot holly down to a stump, sustaining scratches up to her elbows despite long sleeves and suede gloves.

It was depressingly familiar, the story of her life. Of course Ward had other women, shorter and more agreeable. No man had ever put Mary Rose first before, why would someone like Ward Baron?

He wouldn't. Except for one thing.

After Mary Rose recovered from wanting to take Ward's head off, she saw that while Ward may have a wife, she had the He-bean, 23 chromosomes' worth of precious Baron-ness, percolating along in the sixteenth week of pregnancy. A He-bean no longer a He-bean but an honest-to-God fetus, seven inches long and sucking his thumb. The first Baron grandchild.

Instead of torturing Ward, she decided to be a good sport.

A tactical mistake, of course. Ward, like all of us, felt more comfortable when expectations were fulfilled in the most clichéd manner imaginable. Where was Mary Rose's rage?

Why didn't she haul off and bean him with the wood stove poker? Do they even have wood stove pokers? I have never lived in a house with a wood stove, so I've no idea. At any rate, Ward expected fury and got wry amusement. First she met him at the airport in costume, then this. From movies and TV he knew that only the truly demented remained calm when they should be hurling unfair accusations and knickknacks.

Ward got up off his knees and let Mary Rose go, afraid of what she might do if he didn't.

6

At seventeen and a half weeks Mary Rose was scheduled for an amniocentesis. She was in good spirits, considering she was about to have a seven-inch needle dropped through her abdominal wall and into her uterus with no anesthesia. After which the doctor would draw 'a thimbleful' of amniotic fluid (is this really a unit of measure anywhere except in *Rapunzel?*), which would then be tested for chromosomal abnormalities, the main abnormality being Down's Syndrome, uncommon, but common enough to warrant this expensive and nightmarish procedure. Usually a woman invited her husband or the father-to-be to accompany her to the amnio. The man was there primarily to squeeze her knuckles until her rings bruised the bones of the adjacent fingers. Also to prove to himself that if he could stomach this, he could stomach the delivery.

Weeks before Mary Rose had invited Ward. He was supposed to meet her at her apartment and drive her to the hospital. But Mary Rose said she had had it with Ward. She loved Ward – how could you not love Ward? – but she had had it with him. Anyway, since when was pregnancy a spectator sport? She'd invited him to come because he'd begged to come, and now she was angry. When the day came, she invited me instead. We left her apartment for the hospital an hour early.

It was my pleasure to accompany her. I'm not being facetious. Mary Rose's amnio reminded me of my own amnio, which reminded me of my own happy pregnancy. There was a sliver of time between Lyle's adjustment to the unexpected news that he would soon be a father and the reality of Stella's first soiled diaper when it looked as if we were made for each other.

Lyle was very taken with the ultrasound proceedings and would never miss 'a viewing.' During the final weeks of my pregnancy there was some question as to whether Stella was in a breech position, and my doctor did an ultrasound in his office. Even though the blurry white image of her would appear for no more than a minute, Lyle rushed from work to be there.

After ascertaining that Stella had indeed turned head down, the doctor ran the transducer up my belly, stopping at a point bellow my navel. There, through my abdominal wall, through Stella's own narrow back, we could see her heart. It looked like a shell, broken in half and worn by the sea, the four chambers outlined in white, her blood already lub-dubbing along its predestined course.

Lyle is quite far-sighted, and in his rush to make the appointment had left his glasses on the seat of the car. He pushed his way between the doctor and the screen, grasped the sides of the monitor with both hands as though taking someone by the shoulders. I can see him even now, bent over, his perfectly ironed white button-down coming untucked, his face two inches from the screen, his collie eyes wide, frantic to see, tears on his cheeks. 'Is that our heart?' he whispered.

'The baby's heart. Yes, it is,' said my doctor.

Lyle misspoke, but of course he was right: It was our heart. Half mine, half his, wholly hers. It is not marriage that joins people together, but this. And it is this knowledge, and the memory of that day, that makes it difficult to leave Lyle. It does not, however, affect my desire to throw something really big and breakable at his head.

Friends who'd been through an amniocentesis and the men who'd watched all told Mary Rose that it was nothing. They said it the way vets talk fondly about their time in Nam. This was meant to be reassuring. Mary Rose knew it was a lie; getting poked through your abdomen with a seven-inch needle while wide awake could hardly be nothing. In fact, two days after the procedure she was still sore.

The culprit was not the needle, nor the doctor wielding it, the kindly Dr. Karlbom, who looked like an anchorman with good ratings. It was rather the grim, overly lip-glossed ultrasound technician who caused the trouble. Women like to assume that female health professionals are kinder and gentler than their male counterparts. This is simply not true.

Mary Rose and I sat beside the watercooler in the wide hallway outside the genetic counselor's office, Mary Rose inflating her bladder with water from a pointed paper cup.

When we went into the surgery where the amnio was to be performed, the technician came in sour-faced, flipping through Mary Rose's file. The surgery was not in an operating room at all, but rather a storage room. The boxes of medical supplies had been shoved into one corner and a gurney had been rolled in and abandoned.

Mary Rose, trying for levity, said, 'So, how many of these do you do a day?'

'God, it feels like a hundred,' said the tech, rolling her head around on her neck, as if she was already past fatigue.

'So you really enjoy your work?'

Ms. Surly-to-Bed, Surly-to-Rise did not deign to respond. She desultorily flipped through Mary Rose's file, while Mary Rose lay on the gurney in her hospital gown, palms sweating, still believing that the tech wouldn't hurt her if she was cooperative and made her laugh. 'I've got a fibroid. I brought a copy of my first ultrasound so you could see it. Kinda like telling a water-skier where the rocks are.'

'A *fibroid*? Oh great. Is it huge?' The tech waved the report away.

'You mean bigger than a bread box, or what?'

The tech mumbled a number in centimeters, which meant absolutely nothing, our punishment for refusing to learn metric.

The direct reward for submitting to an amnio, is the pre-needle ultrasound. At seventeen and a half weeks the fetus is completely formed and the technician will usually take you on a guided tour of torso, skull, and limbs, pausing to allow for thunderstruck ohhs and ahhs as the baby rolls and kicks.

This dominatrix rolled the transducer back and forth over Mary Rose's satiny belly without pausing to allow us to enjoy even a flash of a view. Occasionally she would linger over some hank of flesh, 'That's the spine, or no, an arm.'

'Oh,' Mary Rose gasped, trying to crane her neck to see, 'look there's the . . . wait . . . what's . . . look, he's waving at us!'

The tech was busy measuring the cross section of the torso when a skeleton hand, dime-sized, floated into view. The baby seemed deliberately to wave its hand in front of its face, as if brushing away a fly.

'There's that fibroid.' The tech clucked.

'When you get a minute, we would appreciate another view of the World's Cutest Human.'

'Who?'

'The baby,' I said.

'We don't have time. What with this fibroid.'

'Do you really need to press so hard? You're killing my bladder.'

'Yep.'

She rolled the transducer up above Mary Rose's navel,

throwing an image on the screen of the baby curled away from us. It was easy to overinterpret. Who wouldn't roll away from the ministrations of the Marquess de Sade?

The tech left without a word to summon the doctor. Mary Rose began to cry. 'That teeny hand!' she said. She was thinking of the unteeny needle about to disrupt the He-bean's perfect uterine home. Or of the fibroid, looming, threatening, an anvil on top of the doorway, a boulder balancing atop a cliff.

Or she was thinking, I have no business bringing a baby into this world.

Dr. Karlbom was as kind as rumor had it. He shook my hand, willing to accord me the respect reserved usually for the father, in the event that I was in some way related to the baby. He then took Mary Rose's hands in both of his and said, 'They call me Dr. Painless.'

'Unlike your lovely assistant on the floor by the box where Carol Merrill is now standing.'

Dr. Karlbom smiled warmly. He had no idea what she was talking about, but recognized hysterical pre-amnio spluttering when he heard it.

Before Mary Rose could complain, the lovely assistant returned. She was suddenly perky and accommodating. Had she been one of Lynne Baron's Labrador retrievers she would have been gamboling beside Dr. Karlbom, her pink tongue lolling, her wet brown eyes desperate for approval.

Though billed as a simple out-patient procedure, amnio has in common with brain surgery nasty tea-colored antiseptic wash, the necessity of a sterile field, and rubber gloves that go snap.

I took Mary Rose's hand between both of mine and started talking about the Blazers, the cement of our friendship. Or rather, it was the two free agents in town looking to sign with the Blazers, but I'll get to that later.

Dr. Karlbom found a triangle of amniotic fluid on the monitor. He tapped along Mary Rose's abdomen with two knuckles, eyes never leaving the screen, until he found the corresponding spot, just to the left of Mary Rose's navel. The technician handed him a blue paper tablecloth, with which he covered Mary Rose, collarbone to knee.

Dr. Karlbom then told Mary Rose to take one short breath in, a long one out, then long lazy breaths. She stared straight up at the ceiling, counting the holes in the acoustic tiles. What would we do without those holes in the ceiling, the pregnant woman's best friend?

I watched. My duty.

'I really think Mark McDaniel has come alive this season. I used to think he was just a bruiser, but he's really improved at the line,' said Mary Rose. Her voice quavered.

Dr. Karlbom held the needle like a dart, and with a flick of his wrist sent it plunging into her. He attached a syringe to the end of the needle and slowly pulled up the plunger, filling the shaft with a clear bourbon-colored fluid. It took much longer than the thirty seconds Mary Rose had anticipated.

'He is a bruiser,' I said, 'which is what they need. Our front line is too effete, too gentlemanly.'

The tendons in Dr. Karlbom's hand stood up with the effort of getting the syringe to draw.

'There is Derik Crawshaw, though. Have you noticed his left-handed hook? It takes my breath away, that left-handed hook. You add that to the fact he's not afraid to bump heads. That's his one true gift. Whereas by the end of the game the other guys will get tired of getting thrashed, he keeps taking it to the basket and taking it to the basket. Doesn't he, Brooke? Doesn't Derik keep taking it to the basket, no matter how beat up he's getting?'

'He does, Mary Rose.' I patted her hand.

Dr. Karlbom filled two syringes.

Thimbleful, schmimbleful. The instant the second syringe was filled he plucked out the needle, disposing of it blindly beneath the table. He bowed slightly and applauded Mary Rose. See? All gone. Nothing in my hands or up my sleeve.

He looked at me over Mary Rose and said, 'If we had babies, Cain and Abel would have been the last of the race.'

I laughed obediently, presuming by 'we' he meant men. It was obviously the line he trotted out for expectant fathers to reassure them that their wives or girlfriends were troupers.

We were again left alone with the sadistic technician. She licked those shiny lips and rolled the ultrasound transducer one last time over Mary Rose's belly. Mary Rose eagerly watched the screen for a final glimpse, certain that since she had survived he had survived.

She was mildly alarmed when his grainy gray-and-white image appeared. The tech held the transducer on the top of Mary Rose's belly, giving us a side view of the He-bean, his back lying along Mary Rose's front, his feet and hands curled up, facing Mary Rose's spine. Only they were not curled up. As the technician rolled the transducer an inch this way and that, pressing hard to circumvent the fibroid, which seemed to always be in the way, the He-bean madly paddled his hands and feet, a crab scuttling across the ocean floor, trying to escape a squid.

In the coffee shop, whose menu choices and prices rivaled that of the airport, Mary Rose couldn't stop shaking, like a victim of frostbite. She drank her milk and ate her sandwich and tried to stop her chattering teeth.

'It was like being pinned to a board by an overzealous butterfly collector,' said Mary Rose.

'Or like being impaled by some psycho gentleman scientist in a fifties sci-fi movie.'

86

'But there he is. He's really in there.'

We gazed at the small square of black celluloid begrudgingly given us by the technician: the He-bean's first photograph. He faced away from us, knees pulled up, so that all that was visible was a dollop of torso and his rather large oval head, and the places where the skull, at that very moment, was being stitched together by an unseen hand.

Mary Rose still felt jittery, so I offered to go get the car and bring it around to the front of the hospital. The automatic doors hissed open, and who did I see striding across the street, hands stuffed in his jeans pockets, collar turned up against the cold, hair blown sideways, big scowl on his feckless face, but the catch-of-the-day, Ward Baron.

'Where is she?' said Ward. He combed through his hair with his fingers, then took some Chapstick from his jeans' pocket and rolled it on.

'I'm fine, and you?'

'I was supposed to meet her at her apartment and she wasn't there. I know she said the apartment. This is just the kind of thing I've been reading about. Women get so scattered when they're pregnant. It's the hormones.'

'Wow, really?'

'I know she said the apartment.'

'Actually she's inside. She should be out in a minute.'

'Christ.' He rolled his arm over and looked at his watch. He wore it with the face on the inside of his wrist. 'I rescheduled a meeting for this.'

'It's nice you're going to be one of those involved fathers. You've been doing a lot of reading apparently.'

'Yup. I've already gotten up to labor.' He cracked his knuckles. 'What's she doing in there anyway, going to the bathroom? That's the other thing women have to do when they're pregnant. Pee all the time.'

'So you must be all ready for the perineal massage.'

'Sure am.' Checked his watch again, combed his hair with his fingers. He had no idea what I was talking about.

'That was Lyle's favorite part. Difficult though it was.'

'Yeah. Well, I've been doing push-ups.'

'Push-ups? Now that's interesting. How do push-ups help?'

'It's part of the whole Perry Neal thing,' he said.

'The Perry Neal thing?'

'System. Whatever.'

I started laughing. I started crying. I squeaked and wept. Ward, Ward, Ward, what an adorable idiot you are.

'It's *perineal*,' I gasped. 'It's to get the 'taint in shape. Get it all limbered up and ready to be stretched as thin as parchment.'

Ward looked down at me, really down at me. I'd never noticed his nostrils before. They arched like that of a television aristocrat. 'What, may I ask, is a 'taint.'

''Taint pussy, 'taint asshole,' I said. 'That stretch of real estate right in between.'

His eyes moved up and to the right, just a little. It was the same look people make when confronted with any geography question. Which is farther north: England or Germany?

At that moment the doors hissed open, and there was Mary Rose. She narrowed her eyes, didn't look happy. 'What are you doing here?'

'I'm on the way to get the car,' I said.

'I forgot whether you said meet you at the apartment or here,' said Ward.

'I already had it,' said Mary Rose. 'Brooke, I can walk. You don't have to get the car.'

'God, I'm sorry. I was late, wasn't I? I thought for sure you said to meet you at the apartment. I'm sorry you had to go through it by yourself. Did it go all right? Everything okay in there?'

Mary Rose sighed, rubbed a finger over the furrow between her brows. 'I stood you up, Ward.'

'You stood me *up*? Okay, you're still mad at me. You're bent out of shape that my divorce hasn't come through. See how little it means to me? I didn't even know I was still in trouble.'

'It's more than trouble, Ward. You're still married.' I could tell Mary Rose didn't have the energy for an argument, and Ward could tell, too.

'What's the fastest way to a man's heart?'

'Don't do this. This is serious. It's not the being-married part, it's the lying-to-me part.'

'Through his chest with a sharp knife.'

'Ha-ha.'

'Anyway, it wasn't a lie, it was a technicality. Come on,' he said. 'I'm not mad at you for standing me up, so you shouldn't be mad at me.' He opened his jacket and moved to wrap it around Mary Rose in a hug. She made a face, but stepped toward him, snaking her arms around his waist beneath the jacket.

'It's hardly the same thing,' I said.

'You have that aftershave on I like,' said Mary Rose, sniffing his collar.

Need I say Mary Rose went home with Ward?

On a windy, wet afternoon, three weeks and one day after Mary Rose had her amnio, the phone rang. The phone had been ringing a lot lately, mostly Audra, calling just to check in on the 'not-so-little mother.' She even called from her month of madness in Puerto Vallarta.

'Well? Is it baseball mitts or baby dolls?' asked Audra.

'I haven't gotten the results yet,' said Mary Rose.

'And you're sure they couldn't tell with the ultrasound? I have a friend at the club who says you look for the third leg. That's a sure sign it's a boy,' said Audra.

'Unless it's a girl with three legs,' said Mary Rose.

'Don't talk like that. This baby is perfectly healthy. I don't know what you're worried about. There's not a thing wrong with our genes. We never had tests like these in my day. All they do is make doctors rich and new mothers nervous. Not that I'm advocating a return to ignorance. God knows we don't want a mongoloid. Anyway, there's nothing wrong with our genes. And after watching you cut down that quaking aspen I'm sure there's nothing wrong with yours. You'll call and let me know as soon as you hear anything. I'm going to buy the crib linen for you, so I would like to know.'

'I don't want to know the sex, Audra. But I will call and let you know if there's anything else.'

'I understand, honey. Keep it a surprise. When do you see the doctor again?'

'Tuesday.'

'What did you say his name was again?'

'Her. Janet Vertamini. At the Cascade Women's Clinic.'

'A woman? My, my, you are modern. In my day it was thought unnatural to have a woman doctor.'

On the day Mary Rose got the news, she had just returned from interviewing Sarah, one of her new Mower and Rakers, and was in the bathroom licking Bon Ami cleanser from her cupped palm. Yes, you read it right, Bon Ami. In addition to the powdery metallic taste, Mary Rose had developed a taste for the scritch between her teeth. This hankering for cleaning powder was the only food craving Mary Rose had during her entire pregnancy. Mary Rose thought it was probably some need for extra calcium, and since there was nothing about eating Bon Ami in the literature she had amassed, she assumed it was harmless. Pickles and ice cream, you see, is largely a myth.

The phone rang. Mary Rose dusted her palms off in the sink and gave the bowl a quick swipe with the sponge.

The voice said, 'Hello, it's Geenie Burns from the Cascade Women's Clinic. Good news. Everything looks normal.'

'Normal?' said Mary Rose. Normal was good, right? Why didn't Geenie Burns say great? Everything looks great!

'You said you didn't want to know the gender?'

'Oh, God, I'm pregnant,' said Mary Rose.

'Isn't this Mary Rose Crowder?'

Geenie Burns, Geenie Burns, don't you know this makes It official? The advent of prenatal testing has made it possible to be only a little bit pregnant. Mary Rose patted the He-bean twitching beneath her belly button. He was a prodigy of gestation after all.

'Ha-ha!' She slid around the wood floors in her rag socks, snapping her fingers. She called all of us: Ward, Audra, even Fleabo. By the time she got to me her mood had deteriorated.

'Labor,' said Mary Rose. 'Now I have to go through labor. You get over one worry hurdle, then there's another. Just like you said.'

'Wait'll the first time you take him out to practice for his learner's permit,' I said.

'Describe the pain to me again. Don't say it's indescribable,' said Mary Rose.

'It's like being screwed onto a fence post,' I said.

'Not really.'

'No, I made it up,' I said.

Mary Rose had heard that labor and delivery was like an athletic event. It's not unlike an athletic event, but the event it most resembles is bronco riding, where the main thing is just hanging on until it's over. Nonetheless she thought she should be in even better shape than she already was and, as I mentioned earlier, had enrolled herself in a prenatal water aerobics class.

It was a little silly – bouncing up and down in the water to show tunes was what it amounted to – but silliness was a small price to pay to be weightless for forty-five minutes three times a week. Some days there were two other pregnant women in the class, sometimes a dozen. The teacher was a twenty-three-year-old who had two children and not a mark on her. Mary Rose suspected this was her main qualification for teaching the class, since she repeatedly had trouble keeping the beat of 'Everything's Coming Up Roses.'

Mary Rose was on the verge of finding another class when she made the acquaintance of a soft-spoken, doe-eyed cellist in our city's symphony. Mary Rose liked the cellist because she enjoyed imagining what she looked like playing the cello at nine months along. As with many aspects of pregnancy, the difficult part was not what you might expect: It was the calluses on the ends of the cellist's fingers that were giving her pains; new blisters formed with every incremental readjustment of the instrument, made to accommodate her expanding belly. Mary Rose was amazed. It was the same with her and her rototiller.

Halfway through each class, when the paddleboards were distributed, Mary Rose would find herself paddling to the other end of the pool and back with the cellist, whose name she learned the first day, then forgot, then was too shy to ask again.

One day, Mary Rose mentioned that the cellist was lucky. Her baby would come out knowing Mozart while Mary Rose's baby would come out familiar only with the sounds of lawn mower, chain saw, and the announcer's voice on Blazer cable. The cellist wasn't totally without a sense of humor, but she was one of those people who needed ample warning that a joke was on its way.

'I'm also reading her the Civilization Series,' said the cellist. 'We're on *The Age of Reason Begins*.' She went on to tell Mary Rose about the In Uteroversity, an institution of 'prelearning' based in northern California and available by subscription. It provided week-by-week 'lesson plans' based on fetal development and the kind of preknowledge you might like your child to have.

'How does she hear you?' asked Mary Rose. 'Being a fetus is like living inside a washing machine.'

'They send you a special device that fits over your stomach, like a megaphone. It amplifies the sound in such a way that your words are quite clear.'

Mary Rose doubted it. She was hardly going to become a subscriber herself, the 'in tuition' being quite expensive. But Mary Rose thought it couldn't hurt to talk to the He-bean a little more, get him used to her voice.

I haven't gone off on a tangent here. I'm telling you this so you can understand how it was that Ward came to think that Mary Rose had finally cracked. No one uses the term 'gone mad' anymore. Most people think it's the word *mad* at fault – too dramatic. I think it's the *gone* that's ruined the phrase, and lay it at the feet of jet travel. It's too easy to come back from where ever you've been, even madness. *Cracked* implies someone irrevocably damaged, and that is the word Ward would use to describe Mary Rose to his lawyer, whom he would bring in to sue Mary Rose for custody of the as-yet-unborn Baron baby.

Now I am going off on a tangent.

7

I'm not sure what got into me, why I felt the need to torment Ward in front of the hospital the day of Mary Rose's amnio. There's always the He Deserved It rationale, but was I the one to dish it out? No. What went on between Mary Rose and Ward had nothing to do with me. I think it was simple jealousy. Ward, feckless though he may be, still raced to the hospital to meet Mary Rose, still wanted to be a part of this birth. He may have been legally married to someone else, but he was absorbed in Mary Rose and the baby. Marriage, like the original definition of the word *gay*, has lost its meaning. Lyle and I are married, and even though I just went on at length about how endearing he was at my amnio, now that Stella was here, he'd checked out. If I had a choice between absorption (despite its paper-towelish connotations) and a marriage license, I don't think I'd take the license, although they are very lovely in our state, with a filigreed blue-black border and an embossed covered wagon at the bottom.

Lyle's hours at work had been cut back just after Stella was born, and now he spent most of his time on-line. He got home from work around two-thirty, and played Realm of the Elf until midnight. I think he had a girlfriend on-line. Like everyone else, I couldn't decide whether this was cheating or not.

Her screen name was Lil Plum. I know about her because one time I was talking to the back of Lyle's head just as he was booting up Realm of the Elf, and an instant message popped on the screen: *I love you, Rtist, where have you been?* Rtist is Lyle's screen name, chosen, I presume, while he still fashioned himself a painter and not a computer geek.

'Who's Lil Plum?' I asked. It leapt from my mouth like a feisty fish.

Why do women ask this question? We might as well just say, 'I'm feeling in need of being lied to. Any chance you could help me out?' The back of Lyle's neck reddened.

'A friend from the game. She plays a healer. She's awesome with head wounds.'

'Lucky you.'

'Every time a musk hog gouges my eye out, she's always right there, always ready to help me out.'

'Is this an InfideLite here, Lyle, or what?'

InfideLite was a word we'd invented when cheating on each other was as likely as income-tax reform. Thus, we could afford to be cavalier. We had philosophical discussions in bed, after having nearly concussed ourselves making love. We'd agreed that a full-blown affair was unforgivable, but an InfideLite could probably be overlooked, in time. An InfideLite, as we defined it, is what used to be called a one-night stand. It happens furtively. There are no illicit meetings at noon in a downtown hotel, no phone numbers changing hands. There are no meals or bottles of anything from France. Marriages remain intact, if strained; hearts remain unbroken.

'She lives in Blue Mound, Illinois, Brooke,' Lyle said, annoyed, not wanting to go along with our old joke.

'Is that supposed to reassure me that you're not having an affair, or what?'

In some ways it would have been better if he were having an affair in RL – an affair in Real Life, to use the proper net terminology. For one thing, he would never be home, which means he wouldn't be underfoot, leaving his wet towels on the wood floors of our bedroom and forgetting to put the milk back in the refrigerator. He would be out, and he would feel guilty, which would encourage him to bring me flowers, take me out to dinner, offer to take Stella so I could get out myself. Since it was only an on-line fling, however, Lyle felt no need to make amends. He still expected to be fed and watered. He expected me to allow him this, since, as he pointed out whenever I made noises about how much time he spent on his computer, at least he wasn't out in bars with other women . . .

The unsaid part was, like I had been with other men.

When Stella was just four weeks old Lyle took care of her while I went out and did a bad thing. Actually, it wasn't really bad. In our world really bad, Dicky Baron–variety bad, gets you celebrity, with its attendant television shows and book deals. What I did was more sort of cowardly and craven: I lied about having been bad.

In a way, it explains everything: why Lyle professes to have no interest in basketball; why he has withdrawn; why he allows Lil Plum of Blue Mound, Illinois, to minister to his virtual head wounds.

The day I was bad had been a suffocating day in late summer, humid and smoggy, the pollen count off the chart. Downstate they were field-burning or spraying, something that made the doomsday-red sky smell like burnt hair.

Mary Rose and I met for a drink in the bar at the same hotel where I had stayed during the film seminar, the hotel where Lyle and I had fallen in love. It had expert air-conditioning, comfortable leather chairs, and fond memories. It was the first time I had been out of the house since Stella was born.

The bar was not crowded. Despite the fact it was 6:30 and

still nearly 95 degrees, no one seemed interested in escaping the heat. People preferred to sit outside. As I said above, we in our city would rather suffer dehydration, sunburn, and heat stroke than appear inhospitable, for fear that next year our few weeks of real heat would go somewhere else. Mary Rose and I, of course, were originally from California, and therefore ingrates. We took heat for granted.

What an odd pair we were. I was then at the very peak of postpartum exhaustion and confusion, fuzzy of mind, limp of soul, doughy of everything except my stupendous corn-silo-sized breasts. I was pale, smelled of sour milk, and didn't care. I had Stella. As I waited for Mary Rose, I held the thought of her in my mind as one might the image of a lover.

Mary Rose had come straight from work. I remember thinking how tall and strong she looked; if she were an actress, she would only ever be offered the role of the beautiful alien from some technology-bereft planet where women rule in teeny outfits, with big weapons. She strode through the dim bar in a grass-stained pair of canvas shorts and a black tank top. She was brown as a brick, her damp blond bangs pushed off her face. She was wearing her Swiss pruners in their hand-tooled holster. No, I must be misremembering the holster. Surely she would have left it in the Mowers and Rakers truck. It's the tough-gunslinger image of her I'm conjuring up. She sat, casting her long legs out straight beneath the table.

I ordered scotch on the rocks with a beer back. I drank quite a bit after Stella was born. Did then, do now. No one can use a drink as much as a new mother. Why the world is full of men drinking in bars is a mystery to me. What do men have to worry about? Money, manhood, the play-offs. The same basic things that bug them at fourteen bug them at eighty-four.

But there you are, mother. For reasons having to do with selfishness and the cruel march of DNA, you have brought forth an innocent who will suffer and die, not to mention figure out that love fades, money can buy happiness after all, and diets don't work.

That's one half. The other is what you've done to yourself. You realize within a week of the baby's birth that you will be dismayed for the rest of your life, dismayed with love. Everyday, all day, will be spent quivering with foreboding. You will ache with the effort of listening. For breathing, wheezing, the slam of a car door, the sounds of muffled crying. Stretch marks are nothing compared to this. You have discovered the fifth chamber of your heart, the cozy quarters where the dismay will reside until the day you die. Your child may die, it happens, but the dismay is unimpeachable.

You will never not be a mother.

And no one who isn't a mother understands this, or cares, except when you do something spectacular like pick up a Volkswagen.

'So it's no wonder I drink,' I said. Mary Rose had eyed my scotch and beer with disapproval. She was then so far away from considering childbirth herself that she could afford to know everything.

'I just heard it wasn't good for the baby, that's all,' she said, looking at the menu.

'No, you're right.' I didn't want to disgust her further by confessing I had pumped a few bottles' worth of milk earlier in the week in anticipation of our date.

For this simple date – drinks, a light dinner, then a movie – I had looked forward to as eagerly as I had once anticipated a college trip to Brazil. The smells of cigarettes, perfume. The snatches of other people's conversations. To sit quietly in a public place – look at the rows of bright bottles lined up against the mirror behind the bar! – and sip a drink. To drink the drink and eat the meal without interruption. To excuse myself and walk across the bar with my arms free, swinging at my sides. To walk into the ladies', where I could sit on the toilet with the door closed. By myself. I could pee, or just sit there, for as long as I wanted. No one needed anything from me. I could take my time in front of the mirror, combing my hair, inspecting the circles beneath my eyes, rolling on lipstick. It was like travel to a foreign country. I felt a wave of home-sickness in the form of longing for Stella. But it passed, and I was glad to be there.

People not residing deep in the motherhood called this Life.

Mary Rose's Caesar salad arrived with unconscionably large pieces of romaine. She was very good at spearing them whole and tucking them into her mouth. All that raking, I suppose. I had ordered a pizza for one, topped with ingredients Lyle would scoff at: barbecued chicken and roasted red peppers.

I did not dig in immediately, so happy was I just to *sit*. I twirled my ankles beneath the table, feeling them crackle. The only time I sat anymore was when I fed Stella or when I was asleep. Otherwise, I was rocking her, walking her, checking for a project and changing her, or just generally cajoling her, the latter of which seemed to require my marching around the house with my knees held very high.

I put my elbow on the table, rested my cheek on my palm, sighed, stared. The best part of all this was being able to focus my gaze on something farther than twelve inches in front of my face. I have heard prisoners say this is one of the most wonderful things about being released; having a bona fide distance into which you can gaze. So there I was, flexing my long-distance eye muscles, or whatever.

I swear this was all I was doing.

What I was not doing was coming on to Lightning Rod McGrew. I may have been humming along with the back-ground music, or maybe even doing a little lip-syncing. I talked to Stella all the time, narrating life for her as advised in countless baby books, and sometimes I got to talking aloud even when I was alone. If I was talking to myself surely Mary Rose would have said something?

According to Lightning Rod McGrew, I was talking to him.

Lightning Rod and Derik Crawshaw were clear across the room. I was ignoring my food, my head in my hands, gazing at him, mouthing something. I think it may have been something along the lines of 'come on baby light my fire.'

Lightning Rod was looking for company. Lightning and Derik Crawshaw. They sent over two bottles of our famous locally brewed ale.

Mary Rose glanced up at the waiter, a flap of romaine between her lips. The waiter clutched the cold bottles between three fingers, an unwilling party to this nonsense.

'I think you have the wrong table,' she said.

'Those "gentlemen" over there,' he said. He said *gentlemen* in quotes.

Mary Rose sucked in her lettuce, craned around, and looked at two tall black guys in ice cream–colored shorts and polo shirts, hefty white high-tops, and white sweat socks clinging cutely to their coconut-colored ankles. Their hands were as big as our heads, their arms as thick as our legs.

'Who are they?'

They were obviously Somebody. By somebody I mean professional basketball players. No tall African-American male visiting our city ever seems to be anything else. I am sure there are six-foot-five African exchange students, six-foot-seven software salesmen. If there are, they are besieged with requests for autographs, questioned as to why they insist on taking the outside shot. This attests to both the limited opportunities of our little city and the many varieties of racism.

Mary Rose turned back to me and gave me a look. Behind her, across the room, Lightning Rod hung one leg over the other and waggled his fingers at me.

'They mean it.' The instant the sentence left my lips I thought I had said, 'they mean us.'

Mary Rose leaned back in her leather chair, crossed her bony forearms across her chest, tossed her head back, and giggled. 'Us?' she whispered almost hysterically.

It wasn't *that* weird.

They joined us.

It was that weird. Of course it was. Lightning Rod McGrew and Derik Crawshaw were . . . I won't say desperate. I will say they were in their mid-twenties, hot, bored, and tired of twirling the paper from a countless numbers of straws around their long, long fingers.

They were feeling adventuresome, let's put it that way. They were stuck here for two days, the purpose of their trip to discuss with the Trail Blazers the possibility of being added to the roster. Lightning Rod was a free agent, having just been freed from his duties warming the bench for the Miami Heat. Derik had been starting for a team in Italy for the past three years. We had never heard of them, which was just as well. Otherwise, we might have acted even more ridiculous than we did.

'You was eyeing me,' said Lightning Rod as he picked up a chair from the empty table beside us and dropped it beside me. Our knees rubbed; all of our knees rubbed.

'Eyeing you?' I said. 'How do you know I wasn't staring at that print of the duck hunters behind your head?'

'You was looking me up and down. Like a pot of half-finished gumbo looks at a net full of fresh crab.'

'A pot can't look at anything.'

'You white girls such sticklers for details. That's what I like about you.'

'I'm sure that's the first quality you look for in a woman,' I said.

'Tell this lady – what's your name, sis? – tell this lady how I like white girls.'

'Our African-American sisters wants to keyo him. It's a fact,' said Derik. He had cheekbones you could park your elbows on, long paisley-shaped eyes, dimples. His voice was soft, an inner-city accent difficult for this average white girl to understand.

' "Keyo?" That hip basketball lingo or something?' I said.

'*Kill,*' said Mary Rose. *This* average white girl anyway; Mary Rose seemed to hear the few things he had to say perfectly well.

'Black women get pissed at black men for being interested in white women, but they forget it takes two to tango!' I don't know why I said this. I *do* know why I said this. One, I wanted to hide my embarrassment by saying something outrageous. Two, I wanted to say something outrageous to hide the fact I was what I had never imagined I would be, somebody's *mother.*

Lightning Rod laughed, displaying a set of stupendous porcelain caps and a large quivering uvula, a word I frequently confuse with vulva. It is uvula, isn't it?

'What you like so much about us?' asked Lightning Rod.

'You two personally or black guys in general?'

'Us personally?' Rod looked to Derik, but didn't give him a chance to answer. 'Let's start with general. And don't say it's our humongous . . . wrist watches.' Lightning Rod cackled. I could see he was the kind of guy who could have fun in an empty room.

'In general we're scared to death of you,' I said.

'Oh, God,' said Mary Rose.

Lightning Rod flicked a glance at Derik. We got us some live ones.

'Even though almost all of the psychotic rapists and serial murder types out there are white, we're still terrified of you. Every black guy we run into on the street who's not in a coat and tie we're convinced is going to rape and murder us.'

'Should we rape 'n' murder 'em?' Lightning Rod asked Derik, who was rubbing his forehead, a ploy to hide his eyes behind his hand. The unexpected turn in the conversation had left him abashed.

'The problem is, the black guy in the coat and tie we dismiss. We got our own white guys in coats and ties. So that leaves you,' I said.

'What about the black auto mechanic?'

'Not interested.'

'Even with a free lube job?' said Lightning Rod.

'You guys are *gods*. You're rich, dress well off court, and look really good on TV. You give away toys to poor kids at Christmas and plead for kids to stay in school. You're the only ones anyone in the country looks up to anymore. It used to be athletes, rock stars, and actors, but everyone knows you don't need real talent to be a rock star or an actor. It's impossible to succeed at what you guys do without having talent. It's one of the last jobs left where skill matters. We *idolize* you! Do you have any idea how many women want to sleep with you?'

'At this table?' Derik ventured, trying to get in the spirit of things.

'In this city! In the country! The world!'

'Brooke,' said Mary Rose. She was embarrassed.

'Now you speakin my language, white girl.'

'Guess,' I said.

Lightning Rod strummed his lips, narrowed his eyes, the pose of someone doing math in his head. 'Five thousand?'

'More.'

'Ten thousand?'

'A lot more. All those kindly, grandmotherly checkout counter clerks interviewed on television during the play-offs who issue public invitations to our players to come over for a good meal. You think a good meal is what they really have in mind?'

'Brooke! God.'

On like this it went, me shooting off my mouth and Lightning Rod laughing and scratching his freckled temples with his index finger. His forefinger was as long as the dowel we kept wedged in the kitchen window, our high-tech security system.

I was temporarily insane. Or nervous, or trying to insulate and protect the gooey new me, the non-wisecracking mom who sobbed at images on the nightly news of a shiny, tiny neonate struggling to breathe beneath masses of tubes and electrodes.

I was also trying to stave off the inevitable. Lightning Rod wanted some action. It wasn't me. Even in my delirium I knew that. I was a beating heart framed with the preferred body parts.

There was some phony talk of our going out to hear some jazz. He claimed he heard somewhere that our city had a lively music scene. He then insisted we go in search of a newspaper. We went to the hotel smoke shop, leaving Derik and Mary Rose behind.

Divide and conquer.

Passing the elevator he pretended to block my way, looped his fingers around my upper arms, pulled me close. I stared into his chest, a vast ocean of spearmint-green pique.

Into my ear he purred, 'I could use some nasty. How 'bout you?'

Infants know when there is discord in the household. Do babies know if their mothers have been fooling around? I would like a grant to study this. I would like to say this was the reason I did not go with Lightning Rod McGrew to his room.

It was more simply the thought of anyone touching me. I had not yet had my six-week postpartum check-up. Sitting down was still a bit dicey. The sight of a tampon brought tears to my eyes. I breast-fed Stella every two to three hours for forty-five minutes. My nipples were so tough you could use them to hang me from the ceiling. The nasty was the one thing I could not use.

'You know I like you, Lightning Rod, but I just had a baby,' I said.

'That's cool. Boy or girl?'

Gotta hand it to him, he was more interested than most men.

'Girl, but that's not the point, Rod. You don't mind if I call you Rod, do you?'

'That depends. We off to do the nasty or not?'

'Rod, I'm breast-feeding.'

A sure way to lose a man's interest is to remind him the true purpose of the female breast. Lightning Rod's long face, only minutes before limp with lust, hardened a little into resignation. It must have been the face he wore when there was less than thirty seconds to go in the game and his team was down by eight. He was decent about it, though. He shook my hand and told me good luck before disappearing back into the bar, the better to hook up with someone else before the night got too old.

This did not prevent me from allowing Lyle to suppose I had slept with Lightning Rod McGrew. I had stayed out longer than I had promised. I came home looking disheveled.

Lyle had been forced to change Stella's diaper four times, *four times*, and he was mad at me. Once, while transferring a dirty diaper from her bottom to the diaper pail some of her peanut buttery product dribbled on his white sock. She was a screaming head of purple cabbage by the time I got home.

'Where were you?' He was waiting at the front door. He dumped her into my arms. 'All this baby does is eat and shit.'

'Mary Rose and I met some basketball players.'

'Basketball players! What were you doing with basketball players? You just had a baby.'

I shrugged. I began singing 'Bridge Over Troubled Water' to Stella.

'What's that coy shrug all about? Did you, you didn't, did you . . .'

'Did I what?'

'You had an InfideLite.'

I didn't say anything. I didn't do anything. I don't know why. I do know why. He was pissing me off. 'I just had a baby.' What was that supposed to mean? That there was something intrinsically icky about me? That motherhood precluded being sexual? I looked at him, just looked. Let him think what he wants.

'I don't believe this. I fucking don't believe this.'

'I am woman, hear me roar.'

Lyle left, slamming the door.

Lightning Rod McGrew wound up playing for the Milwaukee Bucks, and Derik Crawshaw, as you know, signed on with the Blazers. Lyle cannot bear to have me in the room with him when a game is on, so sure is he that I am not watching field goals and free throws, but all those round brown biceps, sweaty backs, delicate wrists, and heartbreaking collarbones. I'm watching both, of course, and therein lies the secret to women's love of basketball.

J.J. Knox, who was famous around the world for his computer-animated music videos, invited Ward to a party, and Ward invited Mary Rose. I was invited because J.J. had done the opening credit sequence for *Romeo's Dagger*. The party was held on the top floor of an old warehouse on Front Street. It was hideously drafty and classically chic, with a rickety freight elevator that had been condemned by the city, and a set of stairs that should have been monitored by some enterprising ambulance-chasing young lawyer. The guests were in their thirties and early forties, almost-successful people who were at the point of remaining ambivalent for so long about the question of having children that it was on the verge of deciding itself.

It was March, and Mary Rose was beginning to look like an aircraft carrier. She could part a crowd as surely as the ship parted waves at sea. On occasion you could see the He-bean kick from across the room. In stores, strangers would look at her, twinkly-eyed, and say, 'Twins?'

She was at the point in her pregnancy when the oversized shirts and sweaters that have been the staple of the American woman's wardrobe for nearly a decade would no longer suffice. The biggest size was not big enough. There was no turning back: In addition to the Jolly Green Giant ensemble, given to her by Audra at Christmas, she had a pair of fuchsia leggings that with each day got shorter and shorter, and a white mock turtleneck with some kind of yachting emblem over the pocket. This was in case the wearer wished to be mistaken for a member of the America's Cup team.

This was what Mary Rose wore to the party, where she found herself in a conversation with a set designer who seemed interested in her to a degree that transcended politeness. Ward was off networking – do they still call it that? – and I hung with Mary Rose. I wasn't very interested in mingling, I wasn't very interested in being there, but I'd thought I should go out, since for some reason Lyle had agreed to watch Stella, and I didn't want to waste his largess.

'Do you know the sex?' asked the set designer, a rail-thin redhead who wore her freckles as fashion.

'I don't want to know. Everyone says it helps with the shopping, but please,' said Mary Rose.

'Pink and blue are out anyway,' said the set designer.

'Which brings up something I've always wondered about,' I said. 'Why are pastels the colors of motherhood? Girls who are already too old for little floral print dresses with a ruffled Peter Pan collar in second grade suddenly see nothing wrong with Laura Ashley the instant they become pregnant. The colors of motherhood should be purple, red, and black. Purple for fortitude, red for courage, and black because, hey, why shouldn't I feel chic?'

'Fuck the stretch marks,' said the set designer. Mary Rose and I must have looked surprised because she laughed, and added, 'I've got three.'

'*You?*' we said together.

'There should also be a theme song that brings to mind not the Teddy Bear's picnic, but the scene where they cross the Sahara in *Lawrence of Arabia*,' said the set designer.

'Anyway, I want the whole experience,' said Mary Rose. 'Finding out the gender at the end is the icing on the cake. You go through labor and it's nice to have the surprise at the end. Although I'm sure it's a boy.'

'That way you don't have any expectations of the kid, either,' said the set designer. 'You don't have a chance to plan their whole life while you're knitting all those socks they'll never wear.'

'If you find out when it's born, all you have time for is to identify and purchase the correct package of Huggies,' said Mary Rose.

This was all by the hors d'oeuvres table. The hostess, a caterer on the cutting edge, had put together a sweating buffet of IndoMex cuisine, all bright curries and ferocious salsa. Mary Rose stuck to tortillas slathered with sour cream. What she really wanted was some Bon Ami.

The IndoMex food was the focal point of the party. The plates provided were quite tiny, so people were forced to return to the table again and again. Mary Rose and I posted ourselves near the hit of the evening, a platter of tandoori chicken quesadillas. This meant everyone who was hungry eventually found their way to within earshot of Mary Rose, who was being curiously chatty.

Mary Rose was lonely, I think. Besides me she had few real friends. Frick and Frack had moved out, as had Mrs. Wanamaker. She was alone in the triplex.

It was especially bad in late winter, Mary Rose's loneliness. Day in, day out, she and Fleabo went their separate ways to rake and mow – the lawns remain green year-round in our city – and in general keep their clients' yards as spruce as possible, considering it was still the drippy dead of a Northwest winter and the only thing that flourished besides the lawns were moss and toadstools.

In the evenings she watched basketball or, increasingly, found herself at Powell's Books, in the Pregnancy & Childbirth section, where she would peek at the books that showed pictures of the Actual Event. Powell's stayed open until midnight. The store was the largest in the country, one of our city's claims to fame, and no one knew or cared if you stood in the middle of an aisle reading a book from beginning to end.

There were always other women there, at various stages of pregnancy, doing the same thing, like men lined up at a dirty-magazine rack. Besides the size of the women's bellies, you could tell how far along they were by the expressions on their faces as they stared at the color glossy close-ups of a woman's usually dusky Sharpei-like folds stretched taut by the emergence of what appeared to be a hairy bowling ball.

The further along they were the less ashen-faced they were. Nature has arranged it so that just about the time the baby is ready to be born you'll do anything to have it done. Even That.

But Mary Rose never spoke to these women, each communing privately with the advice book of her choice, one not knowing how worried she should be about an impending cesarean, another reading up on breast-feeding, the better to alleviate her disgust, and so when anyone at the party asked Mary Rose about her pregnancy she talked. And talked.

'It's really a fun biological adventure,' Mary Rose said to a ceramist who inquired when she was due. 'Like a unit in high school science. They could have girls that get pregnant use their own pregnancies as a point of departure for the study of human physiology. Did you know, for example, that the uterus is the most powerful muscle in the entire human body, capable of pushing fifty pounds on its *own*?'

'I, I didn't, actually,' said the ceramist, clearly not a member of the sorority, nor likely to be one in the near future.

'And the placenta? It can weigh up to three pounds! I imagined it looked kind of like a very red beret, or a huge piece of liver, but Brooke here says it's like a hubcap. When it's delivered the doctor has to hold it with two hands it's so huge. Then he drops it in an aluminum pan like you'd cook a roast in.'

'Ugh.' The ceramist moved away with her tiny plate.

'You have to sign a release form for the hospital to dispose of it. Just like it was any other organ. Some people think it has great nutritional value, so they take it home.' Mary Rose was not so socially backward as to presume this was normal cocktail-party chat. I don't think she cared. I think she thought maybe she was being outré. These were artists, after all.

What she failed to comprehend was that she was being outré in a manner unacceptable to the hipoisie. You could dine out on a really good butt-fucking joke, but mention cracked nipples in conjunction with breast-feeding and everyone moves to another part of the room.

'No way,' said the girlfriend of an advertising account executive whom Ward had come to the party especially to smarm up. The girlfriend had caught the end of the placenta remark.

'They don't – ' she said.

'Eat it,' said Mary Rose. 'They do.'

'Mary Rose, Jesus,' said Ward, making a face.

'It's interesting,' said Mary Rose. 'What's your problem?'

Ward said nothing, steered clear of the IndoMex buffet for the rest of the evening, preferring to suffer conversation in a corner with a young fan trying to get into commercial directing. I caught part of this conversation and knew it well. The young fan's method was not to ask Ward point-blank whether Ward could help him, but to talk about Ward's work as if it were poetry in motion, and even though Ward secretly thought it *was* poetry in motion, hearing it from an inexpert young sycophant was torturous.

Ward kept glancing over at Mary Rose, chattering away in her big bright clothes, bumping people with her stupendous belly while simultaneously grossing them out. I wonder, looking back, if this was the moment he gave up on her. Why wouldn't she shut up? Certainly her doctor must see that she wasn't quite right. Her anxiety over the really very routine amniocentesis, her refusal to stay with him on the houseboat, her utter lack of interest in the progress he was making in his divorce, and now this, her yammering so inappropriately.

Mary Rose excused herself and went in search of the bathroom. It was communal, shared with another animator who rented the space next door. The room had originally been used for storage. A toilet had been tucked into the corner, a roll of paper slung on the end of the plunger. The seat was very cold.

As to what happened next, I know only what Mary Rose told me.

The animator's bread and butter was a popular children's show. Piled in the corner of the storage room–cum–bathroom was a collection of interesting junk that might appear together in a Magritte: a snow tire, a five-foot plastic red chili pepper, piles of old telephone receivers, a green snarl of tinsel, a papier-mâché model of Mt. St. Helen.

The volcano was unattached to its base, a slab of plywood covered with small trees made from pipe cleaners. Mary Rose picked it up and looked through the hole at the top. She rested it on the top of her belly, and it put her in mind of the cellist's megaphone from the In Uteroversity.

'Yo, He-bean . . .' Then she couldn't think of anything to say, which made her giggle. She was in a silly mood, you understand. Just goofing around.

On the shelf above the volcano model, near a pair of high heels covered with red rhinestones, was a gaggle of cleaning supplies. There was no Bon Ami, but there was Comet, which Mary Rose had yet to try.

'Try this on for size, Bean,' she said into the volcano, the base still propped on her belly. She tipped her head back and sprinkled some on her tongue.

'Hmm.' She slid her teeth back and forth, testing for grittiness.

The next thing that happened is the kind of evidence I use when arguing with my friends about the existence of God. If the world was run by blind fate and simple luck, there would not be the sort of staggering coincidences that befall us, which could only have been delivered by someone of superior intelligence with a taste for the practical joke.

At that moment Ward walked in. Then promptly freaked. He threw himself at Mary Rose, landing on her naked thighs – for she was sitting on the toilet while talking through the volcano to the He-Bean and eating her Comet – grabbed the can of Comet and hurled it away as if it were a grenade.

He had followed her to the bathroom, in hopes of having a word with her. In hopes of convincing her, in the most diplomatic way possible, to find another topic of conversation. Instead, he found her trying to commit suicide, talking loudly to herself through the crater of a papier-mâché volcano. Or so he thought.

'What are you doing to our daughter!' he shouted.

Mary Rose stared.

'If you want to kill yourself, do me a favor and at least wait until she's born.'

Mary Rose stared.

'I want you to see someone, a psychiatrist. It isn't normal. Your behavior.'

'Ward, where do you get this "she's"?'

'Oh God, oh God.' Ward leaned against the wall, slid down the wall so he was sitting on his haunches. He snatched the toilet paper from its perch on the plunger and began hitting his forehead with it.

'You know?' whispered Mary Rose. 'How do you know? You don't know.'

'How many lesbians does it take to change a lightbulb?'

'Ward, STOP IT!'

'Mom called. My mother called, okay? She said she was you, and that you decided you wanted to know after all. Then, once she found out, she couldn't keep it a secret. You weren't supposed to know. She was going to buy you mint green and lavender. She'd hide all the pink shit until after the baby was born.'

'You're insane.'

'You were the one in here eating scouring powder.'

'You should be arrested. All you Barons.'

'What "all you Barons"? What's that supposed to mean?'

'You're the kind who conquers indigenous tribes and strips them of their natural resources.'

'You don't know what you're talking about. We're Democrats and always have been.'

'You've been on me since day one and I'm sick of it. If there was a way you could buy me, you would. We should forget pretending we feel anything for each other and I should make you sign a lease on my uterus.'

'That's disgusting.'

'It's true. You Barons are perfect candidates for getting some poor fertile woman to be a surrogate mother, except it would ruin what you like to think of as your reputation as a fine old family. Well, let me tell you, I'm having this baby and I'm having it alone.'

Ward snorted. 'It would take more than that to ruin our reputation.'

He was right. It would.

And it did.

8

Mary Rose stood at the receptionist's desk at the Cascade Women's Clinic, trying not to shout. It was the Monday after the party. She demanded to see her file. She wanted to see the double X's with her own eyes.

The increased circulation of pregnancy had had an odd effect on Mary Rose's normally thick straight hair; it now grew in corrugated waves. In an effort to control the uncontrollable, she'd had it cut chin-length by a hair salon run like a drop-in shelter: open twenty-four hours a day, no appointments necessary, ten bucks a head.

As a result, Mary Rose had spent the past few mornings in front of the mirror trying to fix what she supposed was simply a lousy cut. Her dark blond hair got shorter and shorter. She now looked as if her hair was cut by a peasant mother of the Middle Ages, determined to rid her child of head lice.

The other women in the waiting room were round and serene as wrens.

'I just want to know who gave out this kind of information over the phone,' said Mary Rose. She waved her file in what she supposed was a threatening manner. Several receptionists swam behind the wide desk, darting here and there on their steno chairs. They shrugged their narrow shoulders, avoided Mary Rose's gaze. When Mary Rose asked to see Dr. Vertamini they said she was at the hospital on Mondays, as was her nurse.

'I am not some lunatic trying to get in to see the president,' shouted Mary Rose. 'I just want to talk to my doctor.'

If there was one thing worse than a lunatic demanding to see the president, it was a pregnant lunatic demanding anything.

It's impossible to unknow what you already know, impossible to resnag innocence. We have children for this exact reason. To reexperience innocence, albeit vicariously.

Mary Rose wept all the way home. She wanted to pretend the bean was still a He, but she could not. She knew what she knew, she saw what she saw. XX. Crossed snakes. Longer than any other chromosomes.

Mary Rose wanted a boy. All women do. We want boys in order to spare them the misery of being female, even though we know in our hearts that girls are better. We know girls are better, and spoil our boys because, poor them, they are not girls. It is all very complicated.

When Mary Rose got home she sat down at her kitchen table with a cup of camomile tea and tried to make a list. Mary Rose disliked tea, but sitting down with a cup of it made her feel sane. Every time she leaned forward to write, she hit her belly. When she hit it, she felt her uterus contract slightly, like some helpless sea thing marooned in a tide pool that was the popular site of grammar school field trips.

She let her tea bag drift until the tea was cold.

The list – why she was glad her bean was a girl after all, read as follows:

1. Stella.
2. Girls are easier.
3. If you give a 2-year-old girl a telephone she will pretend to have a conversation. If you give a 2-year-old boy a telephone he'll hit you over the head with it.

4. Girls are more fun to dress. Like I care.
5. With boys you worry about prison and AIDS. With girls you only worry about pregnancy (only!) and AIDS.

Mary Rose remained unconvinced. She laid her head on the table.

For the past two weeks she had been feeling as if she just might survive pregnancy after all. Silly her, supposing she had a grip on the situation, simply because she had passed the hurdles of the first trimester and the amniocentesis. Even the craving for Bon Ami had mercifully passed.

For no reason at all she suddenly remembered something she had read in a magazine. Studies had shown that fathers of sons were less likely to abandon their families than fathers of daughters; fathers of sons felt more compelled to make an effort to keep a marriage together. That Mary Rose and Ward were not married, and that she had technically done the abandoning – all weekend long she had refused to pick up when Ward called, except once to say, 'Don't call me again, you weasel' – did nothing to alleviate what this study implied: Even in this day and age, sons, not daughters, commanded more respect from their fathers.

Mary Rose rubbed the sides of her belly, which was suppose to reassure the fetus. Of what, Mary Rose didn't know. Being a six-month-old fetus in utero was already the cushiest set-up she could imagine.

Suddenly, Mary Rose heard what sounded like popcorn popping in the distance. Outside, it was hailing. She gazed out the window to see what looked like bits of gray beach glass bouncing off the driveway below.

Spring in our part of the country is not lusty but indecisive. All week there had been sleet, hail, freezing rain, sometimes in combination, sometimes mixed with snow. Sleet is rain freezing into pellets of ice as it falls; freezing rain is rain freezing as it hits the ground; hail is precipitation that starts as ice pellets and ends as ice pellets. Mary Rose was the kind of woman who knew such things. What came down now was a confused mix of all three. Then the sun came out, and it was quite warm.

Then Mary Rose heard something she had not heard in weeks: the slam of the front door, followed by footfalls, the rattling of a key in the lock of Mrs. Wanamaker's apartment, or what she continued to think of as Mrs. Wanamaker's apartment.

She got up and went to her front door, where she pushed aside the batik cloth hanging over the glass panes. For a minute there was nothing, then a small man, middle-aged, in an expensive green field parka came from Mrs. Wanamaker's apartment, leaving the front door ajar behind him.

She flung open her own door and went downstairs . . .

Where she ran into Dicky Baron. He was wearing red sweatpants and a pair of huge white shoes with the laces unlaced. In his arms was a box of other big shoes, a roll of aluminum foil, and some mail.

'Ward's not here,' said Mary Rose. It was the first thing that came to mind.

'I didn't think he would be. It's the middle of the day and he's got to be out moving and shaking and making his shitty television commercials.'

'What can I help you with?'

'Nothing, M.R. I'm here to help *you*. I'm the new landlord.'

At that moment Martin Baadenbaum, the man in the green parka, trudged up behind Dicky. Remember Martin? The South African gynecologist? In his arms was a box of new pots and pans. White *V*'s of spittle crouched in the corners of his mouth. 'This weather is right schizophrenic! And who are you?'

'I live upstairs,' said Mary Rose.

Martin put down the box, wiped his hands on his pockets,

and took Mary Rose's hand in both of his. 'I'd say you've got about seven more weeks left. Too bad there's not some office pool I could get in on.'

'Seven weeks of what?'

'Before the baby! I've delivered thousands in my time, so I know what I'm talking about. I like the looks of you. Here's some free advice: Do everything you want to do while you still have time to yourself. Especially activities which involve sitting for long periods of time in quiet places. Go to the library, the movies, church. Your life will never again be the same.'

'It's actually more like twelve weeks,' said Mary Rose.

'This place is really a dump,' said Dicky. 'I think we need some new tile in the kitchen. Some of that nice Italian stuff. And the dog smell. That's gotta go. I wonder if you get an exterminator for that, or what.'

Mary Rose still was having trouble accepting that it was not this nice man with the warm hands but Ward's brother, Dicky Baron, moving into the bottom unit. Our city is small, but not that small. This was surely an impossible coincidence.

'Dicky, what are you doing here? I mean, what are you *doing* here?'

'Big Hank bought the building,' said Dicky.

'Big Hank bought *this* building?' Mary Rose couldn't believe it.

'Its grandfather.' Dicky tapped at her belly. His grin was just this side of jeering. They were nearly the same height, Dicky and Mary Rose, and by this time probably close to the same weight. Without thinking Mary Rose gave him a shove.

'Didn't that interfering cunt of a mother of yours ever teach you that pointing is rude? Anyway, it's not an "it," it's a "she." '

Mary Rose, tipping the scales at two-hundred-something stomped back upstairs in her size 11 wooden clogs and hurled her front door shut. The windows in the front hall rattled, and the air that whooshed down the stairwell blew the hair from the foreheads of Dicky and Martin Baadenbaum and blasted through the mail slots, blowing open the metal flaps on the outside, which then slammed shut, *bang bang bang*. Dicky and Martin were alarmed, unnerved. They were then filled with distaste. Mary Rose wasn't a dragon lady, she was just a dragon. And Mary Rose knew they thought this. And it bothered her.

She had no sooner flipped the deadbolt on her door when she began to feel terrible. It wasn't Dicky's fault his father had chosen this property, of all the rental properties available in our city, to buy.

And worse, she had called Audra a cunt. Mary Rose didn't think she'd ever used that word aloud in her entire life. She didn't believe in that word. Suddenly, her hands flew to the sides of her belly. She hoped the She-bean was asleep. She wondered if fetuses had the same ears for profanity that children did. Tell a child to eat his peas and he looks at you like you're speaking Farsi. Say *shit* when he hoists the bowl off his tray and that will be the very next word out of his mouth.

Mary Rose called me to commiserate. 'They're trying to drive me around the bend,' she said.

'Who?'

'Big Hank bought my building. Dicky's moving in downstairs.'

'Icky Dicky?'

'It gets worse. He touched my belly, that tap like you're public property – '

'I know that tap – '

'And I called Audra an interfering C-U-N-T.'

'Wait, I missed something here. Dicky – '

'I'm still furious that Audra called the clinic about the

baby's gender. I took it out on Dicky. He's never done anything to me.'

'I wouldn't worry about it,' I said. 'Dicky's the most self-absorbed person I've ever known. It probably didn't even register.'

'I called his mother a *cunt*, Brooke.'

'Just forget it,' I said.

'One day someone will tell my child I'm a C-U-N-T and I would like to think that that someone would have the decency to apologize.'

'I'm telling you, just let it go. Apologize if you feel the need, but don't worry about it.'

'You're always saying that.'

'There's nothing else *to* say, Mary Rose. It's the best advice there is.'

This was not what Mary Rose wanted to hear. She was a woman of action, and letting something go was for her rather excruciating, especially when she felt she was in the wrong.

I have several thoughts as to why the Barons felt the need to buy the house where Mary Rose lived. Setting aside for a moment their natural compulsion to invade, divide, conquer, rule, coerce, and squelch, the building sat smack in the middle of the best street in the hottest neighborhood in our city.

It was close in, artsy but not fartsy; you could buy hand-painted serving bowls from Provence at a number of shops within a two-square-block radius. The house looked dilapidated, but the foundation was sound. The plumbing, hot-water heater, and wiring were all new. A new coat of paint, a new porch light, we're talking double your investment. And Big Hank was all for that.

The question is, had they installed Dicky in the bottom unit in order to keep an eye on Mary Rose? It's the stuff of movies, isn't it?

It's true that Audra Baron had come to think of Mary Rose

as a free electron whirring around the otherwise stable molecule of the great clan Baron. The girl was unmarried, unemployed (Mowers and Rakers had never really counted), untrustworthy, an orphan without a mother of her own to see that she took her prenatal vitamins, and bought a matching bumper and dust ruffle for the baby's crib. God and Audra knew Mary Rose could use someone to watch over her. This took nothing away from the fact that Audra was also desperate to get Dicky out of the house.

For despite Mary Rose's baby – a baby girl! Something Audra had longed for her entire reproductive life, but Y after Y after Y, why? after why? after why? had never gotten – some part of Audra had given up on Ward and Little Hank, almost as if, like women, their clocks had wound down and now, save a miracle, children were an impossibility. Her older sons, she was afraid, had become too old to change.

Dicky was only thirty-three, and might be considered good-looking to a woman whose standards weren't too high. He needed a place of his own, but unless he was lured into a situation, in this case managing the new building, he would grow old and enfeebled in the moldy Mediterranean villa on Vista Drive. The job of managing the building also lifted from him the burden of having to find something to do, now that the last of his money from *Romeo's Dagger* was gone.

Naturally no one had told Mary Rose.

She kicked off her clogs and paced. She turned on the TV, but there was no basketball on, not even high school ball on cable. She would have liked to have gone outside and torn out a leggy old clematis that crept up the east side of the house, but she would have to pass Dicky on her way out.

By the time it was dark Mary Rose had settled on a way to make it up to Dicky. She felt he deserved more than an apology. It was not just that she had been rude, the exact accusation she had leveled at him, it was that she had behaved in accordance with the stereotype of the hysterical pregnant woman, the woman at whom the world shakes its head in wonder and disdain. She hated that.

What she would like to do was build him a raised vegetable bed, as she did on Monday afternoons during the spring and early summer for housebound people who received help from one of our city's programs to aid the working poor. But there was already a raised vegetable bed in the small backyard, one which Mrs. Wanamaker had never even used. It would have been ridiculous to build another one just for Dicky.

Remembering Audra's anti-fat crusade, Mary Rose settled on baking Dicky some cookies. She had a recipe for oatmeal-chocolate-chocolate-chip that she sometimes made for her Mowers and Rakers. A handful left them in a stupor, unable to tug a single weed.

Some people are responsive to this type of offering and others aren't. I could bake cookies until I was so weak with age I couldn't crack an egg, and Lyle would still never forgive me for what he supposed was my InfideLite with Lightning Rod McGrew.

Around 8:30 Mary Rose went downstairs. She knocked on Dicky's door with one knee, her hands full with a turquoise platter steaming with several dozen cookies. When there was no answer she knelt, placing the platter on the doormat. She grabbed the doorknob to pull herself to her feet. The door was locked, she noticed. She knocked louder, then when nothing happened, banged with her fist, as she used to have to do when Mrs. Wanamaker lived there. Obviously Dicky was not home.

Mary Rose debated. Should she take the cookies back upstairs? There she would either eat them or be forced to decide how to store them, something she didn't feel up to.

In the end she left them on the doormat, mainly in order to avoid having to kneel again. She went back upstairs, where she worried. Every time she heard a noise, she peeked out her front window to see if he had come home.

Twice, when she was sure it was him, she went halfway down the stairs to see if the turquoise platter was still sitting on his doormat. Once she retrieved the platter, then, halfway back up the stairs thought, 'This is ridiculous! I've left them there for this long . . .' then back down she went.

Her vigil was interrupted during the sports segment of the 11:00 news. Thanks to an unexpected loss by another team in the Pacific Division, our basketball team was now tied for first place.

Afterward, Mary Rose reflexively went to her door and peeked out. The front door downstairs was wide open. She welcomed the excuse to go down and close it. When she did, she saw that the platter of cookies was gone.

She didn't see Dicky for a few days, which made it all the more urgent in her mind that she see him, apologize to him, and, not incidentally, get her plate back. Finally, at the end of the week, on one of those miraculous hot spring days that make you itch to be fifteen again (that's the miracle), Mary Rose parked the Mower and Rakers truck in its usual spot beneath the ornamental plums, which were bursting with nipple-pink blooms, and heard, through the open front door, a television set.

Dicky's front door was open too, and Mary Rose walked right in, a twenty-pound bag of lime hoisted on one shoulder. Dicky was slouched on his new black leather sofa watching a basketball game, drinking an imported beer.

Together, they stared for a moment at the set. It was not the Blazers. They had six days off between games, and everyone in our city was talking about it. It was a suspiciously long length of time. Long enough for them to lose their playing legs. We were convinced it was a conspiracy between the networks, the network advertisers, and the NBA: Nobody wanted us to make the play-offs because we had such a small market share, compared to, say Los Angeles, New York, Boston, or Chicago.

'The Rockets and who?' said Mary Rose.

'Exactly,' said Dicky. He blew over the top of the bottle, failing to produce a whistle.

'I brought you . . .' said Mary Rose. 'Did you get those cookies?'

'Yup, yup.' Dicky tipped the bottle at Charles Barkley, who was pacing during a time-out, wiping his forehead with the front of his jersey. 'People would kill to be him. It was in a survey. They interviewed five hundred kids across the country. One of the questions asked, "Would you kill your parents if it meant you could be Charles Barkley." Sixty-three percent said they would. Even with his weight problem.'

'That's unbelievable,' said Mary Rose.

'I know,' said Dicky.

'You'd have thought it would be more.' She was being facetious. Dicky took her seriously.

'Everywhere Barkley goes, people come up to him. Every restaurant, every golf course. They want to touch him. It's like kissing the Pope's ring. Better, really. What can the Pope do? Even if he pulls out his big guns, prays his biggest prayer, your life might still be shit. But if you go up and touch Sir Charles on the shoulder and go, "Hey, good luck on Saturday. I'll be thinking about you," and then he has one of those monster forty-point games . . . think how it would be to have people think you were the most amazing person on the planet. To be stared at by all those eyes.'

'It sounds like a nightmare.'

Dicky looked up at Mary Rose for the first time since she'd walked in the door. She was still standing beside the couch with the bag of lime balanced on her shoulder, tugging at a bit of cowlicky bang.

'Those cookies were pretty good,' he said.

'I'm sorry about that afternoon,' she said. 'When you moved in. I shouldn't have said what I said. I'm about to become a mother myself and you'd think I'd be more sensitive. I wouldn't want someone to say something like that about me.'

Dicky looked blank.

'I lost my temper. I called Audra, your mother . . . anyway, that's what the cookies were for. To apologize.'

'What'd you call her?'

'You don't remember?'

'You said she was a cunt or something.'

'I'm really, really sorry.'

'Well,' said Dicky, laughing, 'she is.' Mary Rose noticed Dicky's dimples. He wasn't so bad when he smiled, she thought.

Mary Rose did not know what to say to this, but she didn't feel she could leave on this note. She eased down the bag of lime and sat on the edge of the couch.

The apartment was very tidy, bare as a waiting room where few people had cause to wait. On the wall over the TV was tacked an 8-by-10 glossy of the comedian R—, autographed. It looked like the type of thing star-struck deli owners hung behind their cash registers.

Through the bedroom door Mary Rose recognized an expensive weight machine with a week's worth of clothing slung over it.

'Why do you say that about your mother? I like your mother. There are a few things I don't like that she's done lately, things that are basically inexcusable, one thing, actually, but you don't want to hear – '

'Yeah, I know,' said Dicky. 'She didn't tell me you were living here. She didn't tell me this place was such a dump, either.'

'That's not really interfering.'

'You can interfere by not saying something. Ward does it all the time.'

Mary Rose laughed. 'Like how he conveniently forgot to tell me he had a wife?'

'My psychic says it's my family's tragic flaw, thinking we don't have to account for our actions.'

'Wow, she really said that?'

Together, they watched the rest of the quarter in silence.

The panic Mary Rose felt when she realized Dicky was to be her new neighbor subsided. He seemed cool and disinterested, the exact opposite of the rest of the warm and nosy Barons. He was hardly ever home. When he was, he was quiet. Sometimes she ran into him in the morning – he was going to his club to work out, she was going to work – and when she did they exchanged a minute's worth of pleasantries. For a few weeks, it suited Mary Rose fine.

Then she began to think it was weird.

'I am, after all, pregnant with his niece,' Mary Rose said to me.

'He doesn't care. I told you: Dicky's only concern is Dicky.'

'There's no one living in the other unit. You'd think Big Hank would want to rent it out as soon as possible to keep the bucks rolling in.'

'Maybe he's fixing it up.'

'Why are you taking their side on this?'

I then said something I shouldn't have, but I had grown weary of the conversation. I said, 'Mary Rose, I think this pregnancy has made you a little paranoid.'

It was the first time she'd ever hung up on me.

9

Our city lies in a valley equidistant from ocean and desert. When the wind blows from the west, it brings with it chill marine air; when it blows from the east, dry and hot, the unending rain for which we are famous suddenly ceases and we suffer an equally relentless heat. The valley is transformed from verdant cradle to lung-singeing sauna.

It often happens in spring, for reasons beyond my meteorological ken, and tricks our gullible, pent-up citizenry into thinking summer has arrived. We are fools for this sort of heat. We throw off our clothes, the better to blister our pale, sun-starved shoulders. We cannonball off slippery rocks into local rivers that are running high and cold with melted snowpack, and often drown. Shootings escalate, as do beer brawls and car thefts. Local news reports feature the elderly perishing in their stuffy, ill-ventilated apartments and, in the same breath, small dogs left to fry in closed cars. Our normally subdued northern city, a city of readers, recyclers, and basketball fans, becomes, overnight, a place of irrational behaviors and erupting passions.

During this time, on an unusually smoggy Saturday, I asked the back of Lyle's head if we could get out of town. Something terrible had happened and I felt I needed to get away. Mary Rose had been served with papers.

The night before I couldn't sleep, even after I had put Stella down and sung a few rounds of 'Bridge Over Troubled Water.' Every time I closed my eyes, I saw Mary Rose, so big in her final months she looked as if she would tip over, like an ill-weighted sculpture created by an enthusiastic yet inept art student. She had been pruning the Ostlys' wisteria, a noble old vine that had been trained no less seriously than a German gymnast to grow in a manner that entirely covered the lattice above the Ostlys' side patio. When in bloom the dangling blue blossoms created one of those rare settings that look as if it has sprung from a children's book.

April is not the proper time to prune wisteria, but during a boisterous, pre–heat wave hailstorm a few runners had been damaged.

Mary Rose stood with her hands on her hips, her fingers tapping out a ditty on the sides of her belly, trying to trace the broken runners to their source in order to avoid the disaster of clipping the wrong one, when a plump young woman, pantyhose swishing beneath the skirt of her periwinkle linen suit, minced across the lawn.

'Are you Mary Rose Crowder?'

Only the guilty, who have reason to suspect a process server may be paying them a visit, know to say, 'Nope, sorry, Catherine the Great here.'

'I am,' said Mary Rose. She read the summons twice, waddled to where her gloves lay on the patio, knelt on one knee, placing the summons beneath the gloves to keep it from blowing away, struggled back to her feet with the aid of a redwood chaise longue, then returned to the wisteria, where she proceeded to accidentally cut one of the largest runners, as well as the Ostlys' phone line. The plant was half dead, the phone, fully dead. Mary Rose was fired, something Mrs. Ostly, a friend of Audra Baron's, had been meaning to do for some time anyway. It was unseemly for Mary Rose to be working this late in her pregnancy.

She phoned me, on the verge of tears; after some inade-
quate consoling, I promptly hung up and phoned Audra,
promising Mary Rose I would tell her what I found out.
How had such a thing happened? And how had I wound
up in the middle of it?

Audra was businesslike. 'Brooke. I take it you've heard. We
really had no choice. It's not entirely Mary Rose's fault,
although you won't get me to say that in court. But our
baby needs the best chance she can have. Life isn't easy, you
know.'

'Thank you for drawing that to my attention.'

Ward had done what a scion in trouble always does: He
consulted his father. He dropped in one evening around
dinnertime. Little Hank was milling around the kitchen in
evening wear eating graham crackers and waiting for Big
Hank, who was to be, that very night, master of ceremonies
at a popular charity function held every year, an auction
benefiting our city's new museum of science and industry.
Big Hank was a man of many talents, but public speaking was
not one of them. He had consented only because the museum
curator was friendly with a collector who was selling his cache
of British railway watches, and Big Hank was hoping to buy
them before they went up for auction.

In any case, Big Hank was nervous and more preoccupied
than usual. He came to the table in black tie, smelling of
cologne, a computer printout clenched in his fist.

'What's on your mind, Ward?' Big Hank ate only crackers
and milk to calm his stomach.

Ward recounted the recent events with Mary Rose. He
found himself laying it on a little thick in order to assure he
had Big Hank's attention, a nearly hopeless task in the best of
circumstances.

He told how Mary Rose (for her own amusement!) had
tricked him into believing she'd had an abortion; how she had

shown up once at the airport dressed as a chauffeur; how she wouldn't spend the night with him on his houseboat because she didn't want to miss a basketball game; how she blathered on about the most personal aspects of pregnancy to complete strangers; and the topper, how she had developed a habit of eating Comet cleanser. 'I mean, doesn't that practically qualify as child abuse?' asked Ward.

Recently, Ward's eczema had flared up – it was always worse in the heat – and the more Ward talked, the more he scratched, between his thumb and index finger, between his knuckles. The more Ward scratched the more he talked. The more Ward talked, the more desperate he felt. This is another good reason for refraining from expressing yourself. The sound of your own desperate voice resonating in a large cold room, such as the Barons' teak-wainscoted dining room, might make you feel worse than you already do.

And so Ward did. He was on the verge of tears. Big Hank nodded his head, never looking at his son, never taking his eyes from his speech. He wasn't reading, however, his narrow blue eyes locked on a single line.

'Woo! I never knew she was such a crazy bitch,' said Little Hank.

'I'd thank you to mind your own fucking business,' said Ward.

'And I'd thank both of you to watch your language in front of your mother,' said Big Hank.

Presently, Dicky arrived in gray sweatpants and sweatshirt from *Romeo's Dagger*, a towel tossed over his shoulder. As had become his custom, he would work out in the afternoon, then drop by for dinner, often staying until late to watch TV.

He said, 'You talking about MR? She's a wacko. Nice going, bro.'

'Dicky,' said Audra.

'She bakes cookies and leaves them at my door. Then she stomps up and down the stairs all night long waiting to see if I've come out and picked them up. She talks to her television.'

'Maybe she's lonely,' said Audra.

'I don't want the woman carrying my child to be lonely,' said Ward. 'It's not good for the baby.'

'The baby,' Dicky scoffed. 'She doesn't even *want* the baby.'

'I knew it,' said Ward.

'What are you talking about?' said Audra.

'She told me.' It had been a long time since all eyes had been on Dicky Baron. The last time they had all been rapt like this was after he had returned from the Academy Awards. *Romeo's Dagger* hadn't won anything except the Best Actor Oscar for R— , but Dicky had had a nice talk with James Garner in the men's room.

'One day I'm coming out of my apartment and I see her on the parking strip raking up all those pink flowers from whatever trees those are that grow there. She's raking like a maniac, and she's all, like, this *monster* of sweat. It isn't even hot and she's soaked and she's talking to herself, mumbling something. And I come out and ask how she's feeling, just being polite. She looks up and stops raking and yells, 'Fine!' like that's the last thing she is.

' "Better take it easy," I say. "I don't want to have to get out the newspapers and hot water" – that's a joke, like I'm going to have to deliver the baby or something – and she starts to go back to raking, but when she does the rake part of the rake, the prongs, come off the stick. It's broken. She throws it and says, "I wish I wasn't even having this baby!" '

Carrying a baby to term requires nerves of steel. For you male readers it must be similar to how a soldier feels when first under fire. He wants to turn and run, but it's too late. He's stuck in his foxhole. He must suffer through. For you male readers who have never been under fire, you may think what Ward and Dicky and the Hanks, Big and Little, were beginning to think: Mary Rose was certifiable, endangering herself and her baby. Endangering *their* baby.

Now Audra, mother of three, was in the motherhood. She knew that Mary Rose did not mean what she said, that it was frustration talking, frustration and fear of pain. It was clear to her, she of the thirty-eight, thirty, and nineteen hours of labor, respectively, that Mary Rose was simply turning the corner into her third and final trimester, when what looms suddenly ahead is the appalling fact that the only way out of the predicament of pregnancy is giving birth.

I can imagine Audra sitting there, her thin legs in red cashmere slacks folded one over the other, wrists perched on the edge of the table, auburn waves shining beneath the dusty crystal chandelier, knowing she should defend Mary Rose, yet unable to forgive that crack about being interfering. The other half of the remark, the tasteless half, she could forgive. The C word was anger speaking; but *interfering* . . . that was the product of careful thought.

For Audra was a liberal, a *real* liberal, as she liked to think of herself. She believed in 'live and let live.' She had spent her life training herself not to interfere. She looked around the table at her sons. Hadn't she let her beautiful, sensitive Ward live when he had dropped the ball, failing to get his divorce from Lynne? Hasn't she let Dicky live, even though he had helped a young girl – someone's baby daughter! – kill herself? How much tolerance, empathy, patience, and prayers had been required then? She had let them live, and loved them still.

With Mary Rose, the situation was trickier. Mary Rose was not her own, but what was inside Mary Rose was. Audra had tried to be there for Mary Rose. To offer advice, companionship. Some might say Audra was trying to rescue Mary Rose, but what of it? She thought briefly of all the presents she had bought for Mary Rose.

'What am I going to do?' asked Ward. 'I don't think she's fit to raise a kid.'

Audra said nothing. She would not interfere. She excused herself to make some tea.

Big Hank brushed his crumbs from his fingers. He took off his half glasses and laid them carefully beside his plate. 'In our day, children just were. There was none of this nonsense. I have three sons, *three sons*. All your mother's friends were envious.'

From the kitchen, there was the sound of a teapot being filled with water.

Big Hank sighed, fished in his pocket for his watch. 'I'll telephone Ron Toblin.'

Ron Toblin was the Barons' lawyer.

I relayed all this to the back of Lyle's head. 'Why do I feel like a lot of this is my fault?'

' 'Cause you've made it your business when it isn't,' said Lyle. To my surprise, his head turned, and I was treated to the sight of his face, the straight, slightly pointed nose, the brown eyes made large behind his glasses.

He said: 'The game's down and no one knows when it's going to be back up. Why don't we go to Seattle? Spur of the moment. Remember when we used to do spur of the moment?'

That this entailed a three-hour car trip with an infant in a car that had no air-conditioning and a black interior somehow escaped us. We'd missed each other.

Lyle drove while I sat in the cramped backseat singing 'Billy Jean' to keep Stella from screaming. She hated the windows rolled down; too much noise, too blowy. But with the windows rolled up, we baked. Better to bake than go mad with three hours of eardrum-shattering shrieking.

By the time we arrived, Lyle had that tight-lipped murderous look that men get when their lives are inconvenienced by the exact things women are supposed to be born to manage and, nay, enjoy. On top of it, Stella had one giganto project, which, in the enclosed, heated car . . . well, you can imagine.

There is a famous waterfront market in Seattle that appears regularly in tourist brochures and commercials for Levi's and other products aimed at young people with disposable income. It is bustling and lively, and a stroll around it gives people the illusion they are savoring the simple things in life. There are bakeries and flower stalls and blocks of fruit stands selling baseball-sized strawberries year-round. There are outlandish fresh fish marts, where the shopper in search of a modest fillet of sole is sent rushing into the arms of vegetarianism by the sight of humongous glassy-eyed squid lying prone on a bed of ice, buckets of knobby whelks, and tanks of the living Freudian nightmare that is the geoduck, our region's specialty, which resembles a two-foot-long engorged penis sprouting from between the lips of an ordinary-looking clam shell.

I changed Stella's diaper on the backseat – no easy feat; the seat tilts downward and Stella kept rolling off the changing pad – and hauled the stroller out of the trunk and, while holding Stella, unfolded the stroller with one hand, snapping with my foot the joint that keeps it from collapsing, the straps of the changing bag – full of, as you know, useless things that I nonetheless felt it was my job to lug around – slipping down off my sweaty shoulder and catching in the crook of my elbow, thereby pulling Stella away from my chest, where I had balanced her with my other forearm and hand.

Meanwhile, Lyle stood on the sidewalk, reorganizing his key ring.

I felt myself start to grit my teeth. Same old thing, only in a more picturesque location.

It happened thus: Lyle and I were elbowing our way through a particularly crowded part of the market. It was a long covered aisle flanked on either side by merchants selling flowers, T-shirts, earrings, wind chimes, etc. Lyle mumbled something about wanting to check out something, then lost himself in the crowd. I was left there, in the middle of a crush of shoppers, with Stella, who occasionally reached out from her stroller and took a swipe at something colorful and, inevitably, breakable; Stella's two-ton diaper bag, which, as mentioned above, kept slipping off my shoulder, and Stella's cheap stroller, stricken recently with the wobbly-wheel disease that normally victimizes shopping carts. In addition, I was having my period and in dire need of a rest room with a handicapped stall so that I could take Stella and her disabled stroller in with me. It was also, lest you forget, 102 degrees.

When I finally negotiated my way through the crowd, stopping every so often to distract Stella with a toy from her bag so that I might extract from her sweet, iron grip a beaded bracelet or crystal unicorn she'd dragged from its display, I realized that I needed a bathroom *now*, and that any bathroom would have to do, and found a public one, crowded, with no handicapped stalls.

I was forced to leave Stella outside my stall.

Until you have a child, the world of your nightmares isn't fully furnished. Anxiety manifests itself in those I-was-the-only-one-naked-at-the-party dreams, in those dreams where there is a final exam and you are unprepared. Once you have a child, your worst nightmare becomes leaving her in a public place, then turning around to find her gone. You never again dream of being naked at a party; in fact, the idea of being at a party, any party, naked or not, seems the stuff of lovely, voluptuous daydreams.

I went into the stall, and when I came out Stella and her stroller were gone.

For the first time since I first stood up after having given birth, I felt as if all my organs were going to spill out of me. Someone had taken Stella. I knew it as sure as I was standing there. A mother's intuition. I felt my throat close. This was going to be that famous moment, the moment all parents who have lost their children speak of, the moment after which nothing is the same.

On the wall beside the row of sinks was a paper-towel dispenser, beside which stood a short, round woman in a billowy blue-and-green muumuu, drying her hands. When she moved aside, I saw that someone had moved Stella's stroller into the space between the sink and the wall. Stella sat there, nonplussed, sucking her thumb, stroking her cheek with the old T-shirt of Lyle's she'd adopted as a blankie.

Someone had simply moved her there to get her out of the way.

I went to her, knelt down on the old white tile, tried to pull her to me even though she was still strapped to her stroller. My hands were shaking. I couldn't undo the strap, so I just wrapped my arms around the back of the stroller, hugging her to my chest, that large tender head between my breasts. She allowed me to do this, didn't squawk or screech, suffering my love without complaint.

Minutes later, outside, I found Lyle and told him what had happened. How, when I saw she was gone I thought my banging heart was going to bruise itself beyond repair. How, seconds later, really it was only a matter of seconds, Fate decided not to deliver the worst life has to offer a mother.

Lyle has a slow burn, which he stokes by the habit of cleaning his glasses. First he goes *hah! hah!* on one lens, then the other, then hauls out his shirttail – the same wayward shirttail that first enchanted me – and rubs hard enough to start a fire. 'I can't believe you left her. Anyone could have taken her.'

'Lyle, I had to go to the bathroom.'

'You couldn't have waited? That is stupid. That is really, really stupid.'

'No, as a matter of fact I couldn't wait. I had to change my tampon, if you must know.'

'God, is that stupid. That is *stupid*, Brooke. *Stupid*. What kind of a – ' he stopped. He put his glasses back on.

'What kind of a mother am I? Is that what you were about to say?'

'No,' he said. 'Yes,' he said. 'What kind of a mother are you?! Anyone could have taken her. Just walked right out and be long gone.' At that moment Lyle did something he'd never done without my asking him to. He bent down, unhooked the safety strap and lifted Stella to his shoulder. By the curve of her cheek I could tell she was smiling out at the world. 'I trust her with you. Or I did.'

I was ready to let him have it, fling words I knew I'd regret, but his eyes were tearing. He was starting to cry. Now this was interesting. I stared.

'If you're so upset, and obviously you're upset, why don't you take more interest in her? Why all the fuss about her diapers?'

'I do take care of her.'

'When. Name three times. Name once.'

'I did when she was four weeks old.'

'Oh, God, I'm going to hear about this for the rest of my life. Look, Lyle, nothing happened that night with Lightning Rod, although I'm sure you'll think whatever you want to think. I let you think something had gone on because you were pissing me off. I'm sick of doing this all by myself.'

I wrestled Stella from him – using the child as a prop in an adult argument, something I swore I would never do – and left him burdened with the stroller, which, without Stella in it, seemed a pointless nuisance.

10

The game was the second-to-the-last home game of the season, Blazers versus one of those expansion teams named with a non-count noun, i.e., the Heat, the Magic. This has always bothered me. A person cannot be a Heat. Once, I felt compelled to write the NBA and tell them I thought they should feel more of a custodianship for the English language and stick to count nouns, i.e., Warriors, Blazers, Cavaliers.

They sent me a chipped mug thanking me for my attention to this matter.

Unexpectedly, Mary Rose had been given a pair of tickets by a client. It was the happiest I'd seen her since Thanksgiving, when I'd found out she was pregnant. The tickets were not only to the game, but also to the pregame buffet, hosted by the franchise for the team sponsors. Held in the vast basement of the arena, it featured an astonishing array of high-grade dorm food, including a Pontiac-sized white sheet cake urging the team to Ruin the Magic, and a fatty shank of prime rib on a spit carved by an unsmiling chef in a deflated toque.

'What am I going to do? Can you believe this? It's unbelievable. Sometimes I just flat out don't believe it,' said Mary Rose. We sat down with our plates. The room was decorated with four big-screen TVs, providing a direct feed to the action upstairs. Currently, that was three ten-year-old boys in team colors pushing dust mops across the floor. I watched them, preoccupied.

Stella was home with Lyle. It was typical post-fighting behaviour. For a week or so he would try to prove that he was as good a father as I was a mother. Read: He would occasionally offer to baby-sit. I had visions of him cybering with Lil Plum while Stella tumbled down the basement stairs in her walker.

'It's the Barons, Mary Rose. Believe it.'

'I do believe it,' she snorted. 'How can Ward *do* it is what I'm saying.'

'The Barons are the kind of people who keep legal counsel around like other people keep candles in their junk drawer.'

'Meaning what?'

'You and I may think it's serious, but Ward's probably just letting you know the only way he knows how that he's in this, too. Not to get any funny ideas. About, say, taking the baby away or something.'

'I'm not taking her away. He knows I'm not taking her away.'

'This is how the rich operate. They're just showing you their muscles.'

'They just want to reduce me to nothing. They'd prefer it if the baby didn't have a mother, if she could be composed of forty-six perfect Baron chromosomes. Do you know how much I had to pay to retain a lawyer? Three thousand dollars! They're supposed to be so concerned for the welfare of this child. I had to cash in some of my mutual funds.'

'Mary Rose,' I said. 'How can I tell you this? They've called me as a witness. I had to tell you. I don't want you to worry, but I had to tell you. There won't be a hearing until after the baby is born. By then it'll probably all blow over. Maybe you'll have even patched things up with Ward.'

She just stared at me. There were circles under her eyes.

The process server had arrived at my house at 7:20 the morning before. Mornings are not uneventful at our house. There was an 'FBI! Open up!' kind of rap on our front door. I was startled. Stella was desultorily nursing, eyes on the TV, reaching for a Teletubbie, her hand opening and closing like a cartoon starfish scooting across the ocean floor. She was bored, but when I leaped at the sound of the door, she clutched at the lapels of my bathrobe.

Rap! Rap! Rap! What to do? Unceremoniously unhook her, giving her more material for her eventual psychotherapy, or race to the door, bent over, baby held to my ribs, knees bent, like a participant in one of those wacky races popular at company picnics? Stella weighed more than twenty pounds. In the end I unhooked her and left her in front of the tube, where she sat, curiously untroubled, fingering the ear of a stuffed mouse.

The subpoena said I should be prepared to be called to the witness stand after the birth of Mary Rose's baby.

Now I could feel Mary Rose's gaze boring into the top of my head as I nervously separated my vegetable medley into oranges and greens. 'Why didn't you tell me before?'

'It just happened yesterday.'

'A witness to what? What are you supposed to be a witness to?'

'I don't know.'

'You're not going to do it, are you?'

'I have to. Otherwise it's contempt of court or something.'

Mary Rose stared at something over my shoulder. She plucked at her hair.

'Your hair looks great, "Chic." ' I said. It sounded hollow and lame.

Mary Rose pushed away her plate.

'When I was about seven I told my mother I never wanted to have a baby, and she said, 'Why? It's the most wonderful experience you'll ever have.' And I said, 'Because when I get really fat I won't be able to run.' And she said, 'You won't want to run, you'll want to stay put.' And I said, 'What if someone's chasing me?' And she said, 'That's what your husband's for, honey.' Is that the stupidest thing you've ever heard? Someone's chasing *me* and he's going to run? What she should have said is that my husband, or in this case my baby's father, would be the one chasing me.'

Although Mary Rose was irritated with me, there was no question that we would leave the game. In our city people stay in hostile marriages rather than suffer the agony of deciding what to do with their season tickets.

Our seats were high and situated so that we had a nice view of the bench players' bald spots.

'Look, there's the Comet,' I said. 'I think they should have just left it Derik. It always reminds me of something else, un-basketball-related.' The Comet was Derik Crawshaw's new nickname; he was the best sixth man the Blazers had had in a decade, which apparently warranted the name change. Like a comet, he shot in off the bench, destroyed the opposing team's defense, then disappeared (i.e., was rotated back out). Since I'd last seen him (in person, anyway, we saw him on TV all the time), he'd gotten something big and swirling tattooed on his arm.

'It reminds you of reindeers,' said Mary Rose. 'On Comet, on Cupid – is it Cupid? – on Donner . . .' She lost interest in her own joke.

The rows were so close together that when Mary Rose cheered she hit the back of the man's head in front of her. Eventually he moved. Where, I have no idea, since, as I said earlier, home games for the past twelve years have allegedly been sold out.

I am not a cheerer. I'll applaud, sure, but do they really need to be told to play defense and watch for the open man? The men around us apparently thought they did. They screamed until they foamed at the mouth. We were down by fourteen after the first quarter, not the worst thing for our team, who only functions well under nearly impossible conditions. I bought a bag of peanuts from a passing vendor and tried to think whether I'd remembered to put in my nursing pads.

Hanging above us were a half-dozen scoreboards whose sole existence was to offer corporations willing to donate money to the organization a chance to advertise. There was the Budweiser Hustle Board, the Dutch Boy Points in the Paint board. Hanging over center court was the Amerivision board, the main scoreboard and giant-screen TV where you could catch the instant replays and where, during time-outs, dedicated fans who'd brought homemade signs could see their own hopeful mugs beneath their often misspelled urgings.

For Mary Rose and I the most arresting sight during a time-out at the beginning of the second quarter was a boy, his face painted half black, half red, holding up a sign that said: WERE #1! One row down and two people over sat Ward Baron in his big leather jacket, his long legs crossed, his arm around a thin woman with a lot of wavy brown hair, struggling not to lose the chocolate coating off her ice cream bar.

'Is that . . .?' Mary Rose gasped.

Ward, noticing himself on camera, cracked a grin and flashed a peace sign.

'What's he doing here? And who's that he's with?'

Oh, dear. I knew. From a picture I'd seen once somewhere. In a silver frame on the Barons' grand piano? I couldn't remember. But I knew.

'I think it might be . . . now, I'm not sure, I've only seen pictures so I can't say for sure.'

Mary Rose gripped the armrests on either side of her and launched herself from her seat. Our neighbors happily leapt to their feet, relieved that this woman was taking her pregnancy and risk of imminent delivery elsewhere.

For me, they were not so kind. I bumbled over their knees, stepping on toes and coats and a handbag in which I heard the distinct crunch of broken glass. Somehow I knew Mary Rose was not possessed with a sudden urge for a souvenir program.

Ward and Lynne's seats were across the arena, much better than ours. Yes, it was Lynne Baron, estranged wife of Ward, trainer of Seeing Eye dogs, visiting our city to talk about her marriage with her husband, who suddenly thought he might want a divorce.

I chased the stampeding Mary Rose out through the doors opening onto the concourse and around to the other side of the arena. She was running, but I could only bring myself to walk quickly. I was not about to make a scene.

Mary Rose flung open the door leading to the O section and disappeared.

Lynne and Ward were about twenty rows off the floor, behind the visiting bench. The Baron season tickets. Lynne sat on the aisle, Ward beside her. Lynne was pretty, with the kind of thick hair you can't buy, a cleft chin, grape-green eyes. Her hands were folded in her lap.

'I'd like to have a word, please,' said Mary Rose.

'My God, Mary Rose.' Ward sat forward in his seat. He hid his shock by throwing a grin up on his mouth, the same way a person caught naked grabs the nearest article of clothing.

Lynne looked over with mild interest, as if Mary Rose were just some friend of the family, no one of concern. It was clear that Ward had told his wife nothing. She reached up and put her hand on her husband's leather-jacketed shoulder. A cautionary hand, I thought. I saw she still wore a gold band.

'Please,' Mary Rose said. 'Ward, please.'

'I, uh, I can't right now, Mary Rose.'

There is a gesture that only the likes of Ward Baron can

make. The hand is relaxed but not limp, held level with the shoulder. There is a slight flick of the wrist, the forefinger leading ever so slightly. The universal gesture of dismissal it is, bred into potentates and dukes, czars and American men of a certain color and class. Ward did not even know he knew it.

Mary Rose grabbed him by the collar of his leather jacket and hauled him over Lynne's scrawny lap and into the aisle. 'What was *that*? You don't do that to me. You don't brush me off like I'm some, some – '

She dragged him into the aisle, big hands still clinging to his collar in a way that brought to mind the way you might hang on to the reins of a bolting horse. The fans around us clucked a little, but it was too much to ask of them to divide their attention between domestic drama and a little run the Blazers got going right before the half. There were a few *heys!* and a *look out!*, but no one really heard anything over the blare of the music during a time-out and the announcer's ear-splitting blather.

Then Ward shoved Mary Rose. Later he would say he was only trying to get her to let go of his collar. She was pinching the skin of his neck, he claimed. The shove sent her landing smack on her butt, but as she went down, I saw her hit her belly against the armrest of the seat on the aisle.

Between me and the drama stood a vendor. 'Just a minute there!' he said.

It was the same vendor from whom I'd bought my peanuts earlier in the game. He sold small red-and-white-striped bags of old popcorn. A curtain of foot-long red licorice SuperRopes hung from the front of his metal box.

Mary Rose reached back to break her fall and found herself grabbing a handful of licorice. They were encased in thin tubes of brittle plastic wrap. They crackled in her fist. She held four or five. She brought her fist around and began whacking Ward around the head and shoulders. A cat-o'-five-tails.

This is amazing, I know, but check any highlight reel for the season and you will see it. TV adds ten pounds. Mary Rose looked so stupendously pregnant that it seemed impossible she was not carrying a full-grown teenager. Ward cowered. He covered his face with his hands, shiny with pinkish scales of his eczema.

Lynne stood up and said, 'Ward! Stop! Now!' as if she was reprimanding one of her dogs.

Someone on the other side of the aisle said, 'She's having her baby.'

'She's losing her baby,' I thought. All this conveniently videotaped evidence.

Have I mentioned this game was televised?

11

I insisted Mary Rose go to the ER. I saw that bump she took on her belly. As she stalked away, back up the aisle, having dropped the five red SuperRopes, having not paid for them, the vendor not caring one whit – *get that crazy woman out of here!* – I saw her knees buckle slightly once, a move you might learn in a ballroom dance class, her hand fly to the spot she'd hit on the armrest when she fell. 'Whoa,' she said.

Whoa is not good news if your baby isn't due for six weeks. Except it turned out it wasn't six weeks.

It was Friday night, and you'd think the place would be crowded with car accidents, knife wounds, bums passed out in doorways, accidental poisonings, fraternity pranks gone awry. Television ER activity. There was one tiny white-haired lady, crocheting something in cheap yellow yarn. Her feet didn't touch the floor. The magazine covers had come unstapled from the magazines they belonged with, and sat around empty like peanut shells. The magazines themselves gave off that distinct hospital-waiting-room aura: thumbed through but never read by people who didn't want to be there.

A Vietnamese man in aqua scrubs raced out with a wheelchair. I was allowed to come back with Mary Rose because I might have been her partner. This might have been our baby. Our city was liberal that way.

Waiting for the doctor, I said to her, 'It'll be all right.'

Mary Rose gave me one of her black looks that said she had no patience for hooey. She was in her third trimester and had no use for platitudes.

'I've been through this, remember?' I said.

'You haven't been through *this*,' she snapped. Mary Rose had had it with me.

The first doctor who looked at her was a resident or an intern – one of those almost-a-doctor doctors who seem to be there to gain experience not in the practice of medicine, but in the practice of dominating the conversation. He was tall and alarmingly lean, a physique that advertised his dedication to some grueling sport. He smelled, curiously, of bay leaves and garlic, beef-stewy; maybe there was a party going on in the staff lounge. Maybe it was his own going-away party. He stepped between the pink curtains the nurse had drawn around Mary Rose, took one look at her stupendous belly, and said, 'You need to go up to maternity.' It was as if we were in the wrong line at the DMV.

'I'm not having the baby . . .' Mary Rose began.

'Then what can I do for you?'

'Other things do happen to pregnant women,' I said. 'She could have fallen off a ladder. She could have broken her collarbone snowboarding.'

Before I could finish, the doctor backed out of the curtained cubicle. Minutes later another doctor stepped between the curtains, almost like a magic act. He introduced himself as Dr. Deluski. One of his electives must have been Bedside Manners 101. He was younger than we were, as small-boned as a ten-year-old girl. Looking at him, it seemed impossible he could ever have made it through medical school; he looked born to have upperclassmen pick him up and stuff him into a trash can. He wore a red bowtie.

'When's your due date?' He lifted the gown and stared hard

at Mary Rose's twitching belly. When Patricia – the name Mary Rose had chosen – was not reclining on Mary Rose's bladder, or twisting and stretching to such a degree that her mother's belly took on the appearance of a Jell-O mold during an earthquake, she had the hiccups. Dr. Deluski touched the spot where Mary Rose had hit the armrest. There was a faint mark, fig-shaped, not too alarming.

'June twelfth.'

'Hmmm.' Dr. Deluski rested his wrist on Mary Rose's pubic bone and felt for the baby's head. He then asked Mary Rose to pull up her knees, keeping her feet together, then drop her knees open. Mary Rose drew her eyebrows together, disapproving of this maneuver. She'd probably never been examined this way. I stared up at the curtain rings. It seemed altogether too informal. The good thing about stirrups was that no one ever mistook them for a good time. Mary Rose sighed. 'If everyone had a baby it would be the end of the civilized world because after you've gone through this you're never capable of feeling embarrassed again. Can you imagine a world where no one was ever embarrassed? The end of impulse control.'

'June twelfth, June twelfth. I don't think so. Could be wrong, of course. This one feels as if he's already turned. Which would mean you're at least in your thirty-fourth week.'

Dr. Deluski withdrew his finger, snapped off his rubber glove, dropped it in a metal trash can, the kind with a lid.

'Or maybe it's not a matter of never being embarrassed again. Probably what happens is that from the moment of your first prenatal visit on you live in a state of perpetual embarrassment. Breast-feeding. I can't even imagine what that's going to be like. Then it's on to bringing the forgotten lunch to kindergarten.'

'I suspect you're due May twelfth or thereabouts, not June twelfth. Maybe more like May nineteenth.'

'That's a full month earlier,' I said. Duh.

'Back in the fall, the date you gave as the first day of you last period, were you one hundred percent on that?'

'I just sort of guessed,' said Mary Rose.

'You're a big woman, so there was no reason for your doctor to question the size of the fetus. I'm going to send you upstairs for a fetal survey.'

'What's that?'

'Ultrasound. They'll measure the lungs, torso, heart. We'll see what's going on here.'

Mary Rose got dressed in silence, her back to me, modest, out of habit. I imagine she was counting back, counting back and wondering. Back not to when she was in the throes of lust with Ward Baron – you'd think that's what she'd be thinking about, but she wasn't – but back to when she could turn over in bed and not drag all the covers with her. Back when she was able to turn swiftly without knocking over a lamp. To when she was alone, able to read a book in the tub without having it booted into the suds. To when she was a simple individual and not a host organism. She thought back to when there were clothes in this world that fit.

Now nothing fit. I mean nothing. In our city we have several malls groaning with women's dress shops, as well as Saks Fifth Avenue and Nordstrom downtown. There was nothing at all for Mary Rose to wear except one pair of china-blue leggings, elastic-less, and one XXL black T. Mary Rose wore this ensemble to mow, she wore it to hoe, she wore it to do everything else. She washed it every night and dragged it from the dryer every morning. What's love got to do with it? Indeed.

A man's got to do what a man's got to do? Didn't Gary Cooper say that in *High Noon*? I hope not, for his sake. I hope it was some bit player who died of his own stupidity. For it has never been men who have to do what they have to do, but mothers.

Children must eat, they must be dressed, bathed, tickled, read to. That you have just been evicted or diagnosed with a fatal disease matters not. Like the tide, the needs of children never stop.

Mary Rose was a mother, or going to be one soon, and so she had to do what she had to do, which meant getting up the morning after she had behaved in a way that made her wish she could hide all day under the covers, and going out to find a car seat for baby Patricia. You're thinking I've trivialized my entire argument. Car seats! The truth is, it is a law in our state that you must prove you have a car seat or else the hospital will not let you leave with your baby. You don't have to prove you know which end of the baby the food goes into, but you do have to show your car seat. The hospital cares not that your life is going down the tubes.

The car seat and a crib were the last things Mary Rose needed. Although she was worried that buying for the baby was tempting Fate, during the past month, Mary Rose had finally screwed up her courage and began ordering things for Patricia. Tiny pink-and-green-striped T-shirts and short baby pants, caps and socks, a set of hooded bath towels. This may have been Mary Rose's first twitch of the famous nesting urge. Not everyone experiences it.

Lyle, who folds his shirts before he puts them in the dirty clothes hamper, looked forward to this from the day I confessed I was pregnant. Poor Lyle. Every time I put away the laundry he rushed to my side and said, 'Is this it? The hubcaps on the Volvo could use a once-over with a toothbrush.'

The closest I ever came was clipping and filing articles on Thailand from the travel section.

Once the baby clothes began arriving, and Fate yawned, untempted, Mary Rose rolled up her sleeves and started dialing in earnest. The UPS man stumbled up the steps, hidden behind a tower of boxes and brown mailing bags.

There were dozens of diaper wraps, a collection of matching plastic bibs. A play yard. A stroller. A tape to calm crying and a Geiger counter-like gadget designed to detect a wet diaper. This thing that had taken up so much space inside her would now take up space in the world. It was the beginning of Patricia's leaving her. She marveled, teary-eyed.

Ward, on the other hand, did what he pleased, then passed it off as something he had to do. The day after Ward suffered his whipping at the hands of Mary Rose, he never considered that he may have been, in part, responsible. Indeed, now that Ward could officially claim the title of Injured One, everything he had done to provoke Mary Rose had become preemptive actions he was happy to have taken. His custody suit, his parading Lynne in public when everyone in his circle and his parents' circle supposed Mary Rose was his girlfriend, his final arrogant dismissive gesture that gave Mary Rose's fury its head, all seemed entirely justified. For Mary Rose was the unstable one. He, Ward, was just trying to keep his life together and make a good home for his soon-to-arrive daughter.

Even the nurse said so. The nurse with hands that smelled of roses, who instructed him on the wearing of his eye patch – the sharp end of one of the plastic sleeves encasing the licorice SuperRope had scratched his cornea – had seen the attack on the nightly news, heard his side as she ministered to him, and said he was one brave guy.

Even Lynne, who drove Ward's Porsche back to his houseboat, where she put ice on his eye and stroked his brown curls, now rather long, said that if Mary Rose was one of her Labradors she would be put down, pregnant or not.

Only Audra did not coddle and cajole. The next morning on the telephone, when Ward complained that Mary Rose had humiliated him, Audra said, 'No, honey, you humiliated you. It was all over the TV. Mrs. Deets called this morning. So did

Cubby Fleischer. They thought Mary Rose was upset because you had stepped out on her. They found it hugely amusing that you were so stupid to get caught like that. Right on television. Cubby said you could do with a few pointers.'

'But Lynne is my *wife*,' Ward sputtered.

'Spare me, Ward. Have you forgotten who you're talking to?'

'I'm only doing what I have to do,' said Ward.

'I knew we shouldn't have gone ahead with this lawsuit,' said Audra. 'This is not the way people like us do business. No wonder Mary Rose is upset.'

'I don't have to listen to this women-sticking-together bullshit,' said Ward, and jabbed the END button on his cell phone. Cell phones have ruined forever hanging up in a huff.

Ward was at Starbucks, having a midmorning cappuccino. I was sitting across from him, at a tiny table near the window. 'Excuse me,' he said. 'That was my mother.'

'And that's the way you talk to your mother? Tsk-tsk.'

Stella sat next to me in a wooden high chair, pointing out all the dogs. *Dog* was her first word, her only word, and with it came the feminine need to entertain and grease the wheels of conversation. Every time she saw a dog she pointed and said, '*Dug.*' What kind of accent was that? It didn't even have to be a real dog; dogs on billboards, on T-shirts, teapots, book jackets. Once she pointed out a pair of silver schnauzers dangling from the ears of a woman ahead of us in line at the market. '*Dug.*'

She took her pruny thumb from her mouth and pointed at a coffee mug on display. *Dug.*

Ward had phoned me. That was my excuse. Mary Rose wasn't, at the moment, returning her calls as quickly as she once did, and Ward had called me. Ostensibly to see how Mary Rose was doing, since she had stopped returning his calls the day she'd been served with papers; really, to give me his own excuses. Is it still an excuse if you've managed to make yourself believe it? Or does your own gullibility, your ability to pull one over on yourself, transform it into a reason? In any case, I could tell he'd hoarded them, kept them like assets, like a stock portfolio. Stories for the future, when he would need them, and felt he needed them now.

'I am not a bad guy.' He warmed his hands around the squat white cup. His eye patch made him even better-looking. Before he was just average handsome; the patch made people stare, and staring, they realized what they were looking at. Movie-star hair. Small scar, a beguiling white parenthesis, on the chin. Pianist's hands. A man in a leather jacket who reminded no one of Fonzie.

'I admit, I didn't get the divorce because it seemed easier not to. Lynne is high-strung – that's a good word for it – she gets upset. Really upset. Threatening-to-jump-off-a-bridge upset. So why push it? I wasn't seeing anyone seriously, wasn't dating anyone. Plus, who wants a marriage to end? We seemed to get along when we weren't living together, so we thought, well, maybe we'd give it a shot sometime in the future. If I'm guilty of anything here, it's taking the path of least resistance.'

'Did anyone use the word *guilty*? I think the only word we're using here is *dog*.'

'There was no reason for her to attack me. I haven't done anything wrong. That's the thing with you women. You accuse accuse accuse, so we figure, we guys figure, I might as well do it, since I've been accused of it.'

'Do what? What are we talking about here?'

'Then when Mary Rose and I got pregnant, there was no way I could tell Lynne. You knew she had a baby. It died.'

'Oh, God, Ward, I'm so so sorry.' Why hadn't I heard of this before? Audra, information specialist, certainly would have told me. Death of a child trumps everything, explains everything. Now Ward was not simply misunderstood, but tragic. Homeric. I thought I might have to fall in love with him myself. He was my third cousin, give or take. That could work.

'Not my kid, no. It was with her first husband. Elroy, I think his name was. The husband, not the baby. He was in the film business too, come to think of it. Something below the line – sound, maybe? I think it was SIDS. Can't remember.'

Ward suddenly shrunk back into his pre-Homeric self. Old dissembling Ward. Not that the situation wasn't terrible, it was, but it wasn't his situation. Wasn't his baby, wasn't even his step-baby. Couldn't even remember the poor thing's name. He'd just remembered it recently, I could tell.

'I don't mean to be rude, here, but what's your point, Ward?'

'Lynne obviously wondered who Mary Rose was – '

'You hadn't told her *anything?*'

'*Dug,*' said Stella, pointing over Ward's shoulder at a Jack Russell being tethered by its owner, a woman in bicycle shorts and Gore-Tex windbreaker, to the bicycle rack just outside.

'Dog, sweetie,' I said. 'Dog.' I adjusted her blue felt beret and sighed. It was probably the last time in her life she'd look good in a hat.

'Well, she knows now. She knows, and she wants a divorce.'

'That's convenient.'

'I don't think Mary Rose will have me, is the point.'

'Ward, I gotta tell ya. This is none of my business. As Lyle has told me about a thousand times. But what in the fuck do you think you're doing? You're taking a woman you allegedly love, or want to marry, or whatever, to court for custody of her baby, a baby that isn't even born yet. That's hardly being a supportive birth partner.'

'Mary Rose has been acting bizarre, Brooke. You have to

grant me that. And I was worried. For the health of the baby. Don't I have to do what's right for the child? Isn't that what all the courts are always going on about? Doing what's best for the kid? Anyway, the suit was Big Hank's idea.'

'How old are you, Ward, forty?'

'Brooke, it's Big Hank. It's my father.'

'So wait, you want to patch things up with Mary Rose and sue her at the same time? I'm not following.'

'I don't know,' said Ward. 'I thought maybe you'd have some ideas.'

'Ideas? Like what? Like, don't be such a jerk? That would be a good one for starters.'

'*Dug-dug. Dug-dug.*' Stella laughed at her linguistic discovery, which made her laugh some more, which made me laugh, which made Ward smile, which made Stella's eyebrows shoot up, surprised. '*Duggie.*' She pointed at Ward.

'You're probably right, Stella-girl.' He took her pointing hand, her thumb shiny from sucking, smoothed it out flat, then turned her wrist so it was facing skyward. She stared at him, fascinated. He tiptoed his first two fingers around her cushiony little palm.

'All around the garden walked the little bear. One step' – he took one giant tiptoe to the inside of her elbow – 'two step' – he took another tiptoe to the top of her arm – 'tickle under there!' – then swooped his fingers around and tickled her in the armpit.

Stella shrieked with glee. People turned and looked; those in the mood to, smiled. I wonder if they thought we were a family. I felt that weird pang: Ward was a schmuck, but Ward was good with kids. He wanted to be a father.

Stella offered him half of her gummed biscotti.

At 8:00 A.M. a week after the game, Mary Rose and I went to the Vivian Clair School for Girls annual rummage sale.

The Vivian Clair rummage sale is hugely popular in our city. In other cities with less rain, the wealthy put their five-thousand-dollar damask sofas out on the street with the garbage. Here they donate it to the Vivian Clair rummage sale. Mary Rose was hoping to find a solid wooden crib for under a hundred dollars. I was hoping to find a Van Gogh that someone had inadvertently given away with their daughter's Spice Girls poster.

Mary Rose was in a quiet, crabby mood, almost as if she was hungover. She sat in my car, her callused hands upturned on her thighs. Her china-blue leggings were now halfway up her calves. Her socks were mismatched, her shoelaces untied. The sight of her untied laces made me suddenly sad. When you live alone there is no one to tie your shoes.

Mary Rose leaned her head against the window, then drew hatch marks in the oval of grease left by her forehead.

Apropos of nothing she said, 'Do you think Dicky is dangerous?'

'Other than dangerously dull, you mean?'

'I opened the door the other day and he was standing there, right on my front mat, just standing there. Didn't look like he was about to knock or anything. I had been on the phone with Dr. Vertamini, telling her about what Dr. Deluski said. I'd say he was eavesdropping, but why should he care?'

Icky Dicky. I was happy to gossip about poor Dicky. It distracted me from worrying whether I should tell Mary Rose I'd seen Ward. I opted for a one-woman show, instead. I told her about the time Dicky got caught stealing a tape at a local video store.

The store was a one-time Tastee Freeze with black wrought-iron bars on the windows. Dicky had stopped to see if they had any copies of *Romeo's Dagger*. This was apparently a regular practice. The few seconds of joy he felt at seeing three copies of the film in stock were dampened by the fact that none was rented out. The clerk, a blond girl with greasy plum-colored lipstick, was talking on the phone. He slipped one of the tapes from behind the box and put it in the pocket of his raincoat, thinking that when they did their next inventory they would say, 'Wow! Someone thought this movie was so fantastic it was worth stealing!'

'He went through the metal detector and the alarm went off. The rent-a-cop on duty came over and expected Dicky to have a copy of *May the Breast Man Win* in his pocket or something sleazy, but there was *Romeo's Dagger*. The rent-a-cop laughed, *laughed*. Dicky told him he was just trying to further his career. Is that pathetic or what?'

That was how you always ended a Dicky story. Is that pathetic? Pathetic!

Mary Rose sighed and rubbed her eyes with the knuckles of her index fingers. 'Boy, I could use a cigarette.'

At the Vivian Clair rummage sale, Mary Rose and I went our separate ways. I found a plastic giraffe rocking horse for Stella, and Mary Rose found her crib.

It was painted white with spool-turned slats. It had been taken apart down to washers, bolts, and unidentifiable parts destined to be left over when the crib was reassembled. It leaned against the end of a long table of baby and toddler clothes. A ripped cellophane bag with all the hardware was taped to the headboard. I found Mary Rose kneeling beside it on the concrete floor. On either side of her, women pawed through stacks of beautiful dresses, barely worn, dresses they would buy for their girls, who would also never wear them. Mary Rose was carefully counting out all the screws and springs. Suddenly, I felt bad. She should buy Patricia a new crib. Ward should buy Patricia a new crib.

'You'll need an instruction manual to put that thing back together!' I said.

She looked up, straight into my face. 'I beg your pardon, but you have no idea what I need.'

She stood back up.

'What's that about?' I said.

'I'm just tired,' she said. I knew it was a lie.

12

When Mary Rose realized Patricia was going to be born in three weeks, not seven, she got quiet. I thought it was the shock. The Mother of All Pain would be upon her much sooner than she had expected. She wasn't ready, but she had no choice.

Month Ten. It's not nine months we're with child, but ten. Forty weeks.

Force ten from Chromosome. I want someone to make a movie.

Month Ten, when, like a prisoner of war being driven berserk by the most subtle of tortures, you are afforded no comfortable position.

When standing is worse than sitting is worse than lying down.

When sleep, so desperately needed, is out of the question, tormented as you are by the need to pee and the twisting and rolling of the baby, who wants to party the instant you are still.

When the Braxton-Hicks contractions, the alarming and painful warm-up exercises performed by your uterus day and night, no less enthusiastic for its upcoming task than a linebacker in a Nike commercial, strike terror in your heart, convincing you This Is It (it isn't; far from it).

When you can no longer fit behind the wheel of a car.

When, after the baby drops, your belly button is dragged from sight, staring eyeless down at your newly splayed toes. When the baby's heels sometimes kick between your breasts to a degree that put you in mind of water brought to a full boil. When, during increasingly frequent trips to the loo, tearful with the urge to go, you are able to squeeze out three drops (your bladder, wedged into a teeny corner of your torso, has also gone into shock).

When you realize once and for all that you did not sign up for this, and could you please return to your old self as soon as possible? You refuse to believe it is a one-way turnstile; or if it is one-way, that you can't simply turn around and hop back over. Your old self is of course just that: your old self. You are at the brink. You are at the shores of motherhood. You are about to hit the beach. You think you will die. And you will. You will never be yourself again. Motherhood is for women what war is for men. When they had more wars, more men knew what it was like to be a woman on the verge of being a mother, to be at an absolute point of no return.

Mary Rose, who supposed she was only in Month Nine, would now go into labor without the psychological advantage of arriving at the brink. She would imagine there was still perhaps some way she could finagle her way out of what lay ahead.

She must have been terrified.

Then, of course, May 19, Mary Rose's revised due date came and went, and still Mary Rose did not go into labor. She was going to be early; now she was late. This opened her up to advice from mothers and involved fathers from far and wide.

Eat spicy food, then run up a flight of stairs.

Go dancing.

Drink olive oil.

Drink castor oil.

Fleabo, in an uncharacteristically frisky moment, leered beside her as they stood in a drizzle pinching the spent flowers from Mrs. Lemann's prize pink azaleas. He said he heard that intercourse did the trick. He tried to tickle her.

'Another male fantasy bites the dust,' she said.

May 20. Nothing.

Once, she was awakened in the night by a serpentine cramp that surfaced in her lower back, wrapped itself around her abdomen, then squeezed down her thighs. That was all.

In the books they say that being late is cause for despair. Such a limp emotion never touched Mary Rose's heart. Murderous, was more like it.

Mary Rose had her usual prenatal appointment on Wednesday, May 16. So far she had gained a total of 46 pounds. Her blood pressure was 143/86. Patricia was 9 pounds, at least, and growing by a pound a week. Mary Rose's belly was no longer balloonlike, but looked more like a piano covered by a blanket; the baby all knees, elbows, heels, and head.

'Let's get this show on the road,' said Dr. Vertamini finally, and scheduled Mary Rose for an induction.

There were risks.

Mary Rose was admitted into the hospital at 12:16 A.M., Friday, May 21, an hour normally associated with red-eye flights to the other side of the country. The curiously late hour was not for Mary Rose's benefit, a soon-to-be-laboring mother with a top-of-the-line health insurance policy for which she had paid astronomical premiums for many years, but for the benefit of the insurance company. Of course. The hospital charged by the day, as do all American hospitals. Woe to the woman in active labor who asks to be admitted at 11:30 P.M. She will just have to keep her knees together until 12:01.

But Mary Rose was not in active labor when she was admitted at 12:16 A.M. She was grumpy and restless. It was a cool and misty night, raining in fits and starts.

On the third floor, in the labor and delivery wing, there was a board over the nurse's station. It announced how many women were in labor, and how many babies had been born that day. It announced that the Blazers were now the Western Conference Champs, having defeated the Utah Jazz in three of five. Go Blazers!

At 12:16 A.M., there were eleven women laboring, the number of newborns too long to count at a glance. I tried to count back ten months and concluded that despite the heat, people like to get it on in August. Maybe it's the two-week vacation.

A stocky nurse with an old perm led us to one of the labor/ delivery suites and, reporting that an emergency C-section was underway, hurried out.

We stood around. Mary Rose lowered herself onto the chintz-covered love seat. She pointed at a watercolor on the wall, an impressionistic French seaside village, with sail-boats, sidewalk cafés, and men in berets.

'That will help my labor go much easier, don't you think?'

'You can pretend you're having a baby in an art museum.'

The actual induction wouldn't begin until the next morn-ing. The purpose of early admission was so that Mary Rose's cervix might be made more 'favorable' by a direct application of prostaglandin gel. A favorable cervix was a happy cervix, soft and pliable, ready for the rush of Pitocin that would be administered through an IV drip. In normal labor, that is, labor that is not induced, the contractions begin and build gradually, sonata-like. Mary Rose's fuel-injected contractions would start in a manner resembling an Indy racecar roaring away from the starting line. She would scream for the an-esthesiologist.

Another nurse appeared waving an enormous plastic syr-inge that looked suited only for shooting grout around the bathtub. The prostaglandin.

'That's going up me?' said Mary Rose. She had expected a discreet and tasteful suppository.

'Pee now or forever hold your peace.'

I left Mary Rose, returning a little after seven the next morning with the Laboring Mother's Survival Kit: a sack lunch (packed by Lyle, who remembered how hungry he had been, hungry and loath to leave my side); a tennis ball for massaging Mary Rose's back; a paper bag for her to blow into to prevent hyperventilation; a half-dozen sugar-free lollipops for reasons I could never fathom.

Agreeing to an induction is also agreeing to be hooked up to a fetal monitor, which means you are stuck in a bed as soft and inviting as a dining room table for hours, if not days. When I walked in, the nurse was adjusting the straps around Mary Rose's belly – one tracked the fetal heartbeat, the other Mary Rose's contractions. Mary Rose lay on her side, head cradled in the crook of her arm, her not-fit-for-human-apparel hospital gown hiked up to her ribs, her feet, in turquoise sweat socks, hanging off the end of the bed. In addition to being hard, the beds were also designed for women who were five-foot-six.

'How'd you sleep?'

'I was supposed to sleep? I thought I was supposed to lie here and suffer for being a descendent of Eve,' said Mary Rose.

The prostaglandin had caused enough cramping to prevent Mary Rose from dozing. When the night nurse came at 3:00 A.M. to read the fetal monitor, the faint blue scratches on the paper scroll could only be read in the fluorescent glare of the overhead light. Mary Rose's hips ached. Her back ached. No one had instructed her on how to call a nurse. There was some kind of remote control dangling from the head of the bed, but this was for the TV. Once turned on, it could only be turned off manually.

Another nurse, a mumbler named Laurie or Leslie, came in and told Mary Rose that she was not her labor nurse, but that her labor nurse would arrive first thing in the morning. The doctor on call would then arrive to check Mary Rose. Then, if everything looked good, they would be able to begin the Pitocin drip.

'If everything looks good? I thought it was all set.'

'Provided the prostaglandin worked.'

'And if it didn't?'

'We'll cross that bridge, shall we? In the meantime, you can take a shower.'

'My last cigarette, huh?'

'No. No smoking on account of the oxygen.'

'It was a joke,' she said. 'A bad joke, but a joke nonetheless.'

'I'll check your cervix after your shower to see where we are.'

I sat on the love seat and read an article in *Vogue* on the return of the crocheted shoulderbag, while Laurie or Leslie stuck her rubber-gloved index finger up Mary Rose until her hand threatened to disappear. Mary Rose yawned. She was still only dilated one centimeter, ten being the number to which all laboring women aspire.

This didn't seem very encouraging, considering how severe the prostaglandin-inspired cramps had been. Laurie or Leslie didn't think so either.

The doctor on call was someone named Dr. Madboy, not the most comforting of names. He introduced himself, displaying a ferocious, big-toothed smile, his gums receding and puffy. The obstetrician with gingivitis. As a doctor, you think he'd be hip to the importance of flossing. I felt a haiku coming on.

'Should we give her another six hours with the prostaglandin?' Laurie or Leslie asked Dr. Madboy, his hand resting on Mary Rose's side as if it were a fender. 'Her cervix is still unfavorable.'

'What kind of a name is Madboy?' I asked. Everyone ignored me.

'It's all my fault,' said Mary Rose. 'I've spent all these months trying to keep her in there, now she won't come out.'

I laughed, since everyone ignored her, too.

Dr. Madboy ordered another round of prostaglandin. I went downstairs for a cup of coffee, and bought a stuffed duggie in the gift shop for Stella.

I returned just in time to watch Mary Rose receive a needle inside her left wrist. Her labor nurse had finally come on and was preparing Mary Rose to receive the IV. The nurse was in her fifties, gum-cracking and weathered, wearing a number of pins on the lapel of her smock. One said: NEED DRUGS? ASK ME! I don't think it was hospital-issue. Her name was Betty; her gum, Juicy Fruit.

Betty shuffled out to get the bottle of Pitocin. Mary Rose stared at her wrist, a piece of white paper tape holding the IV in place. 'This hurts,' she said. 'Is it supposed to?'

'It's because the skin is so tender,' I said.

'Betty said it was because the skin was so tough.'

'That, too.' I said.

At 9:00 A.M. Pitocin drip began. A bottle of clear fluid hung upside-down in a metal frame posted at Mary Rose's shoulder. An infusion pump released the drug into the narrow tube connected to her wrist one drip at a time. We watched the drip as though any minute it might say something we might want to write down.

Mary Rose still had no idea that between the excruciating moments, labor could actually be quite boring.

Outside Mary Rose's labor/delivery suite – it must be called a suite because there's a Jacuzzi in the bathroom – people rushed back and forth on soft-soled shoes. Considering the number of women laboring up and down the hallway, there wasn't much groaning and shrieking. Either the acoustics were great or everyone was up on their breathing techniques, which, incidentally, do nothing to ease the pain and do everything to keep you from embarrassing yourself by shrieking at your husband: 'Kill me now, asshole!'

While we were waiting for Mary Rose's contractions to start, Ward appeared in the doorway. He'd gotten his hair cut too short, and the movie-star forelock stuck out at an odd angle, dorky, not beguiling. He wore a white T-shirt from a Seattle film-developing company that had a stick drawing of a person holding a movie camera that said, in a child's endearingly lousy print: *Why grow up when you can make movies?* He ducked his head, cowed a little by all the medical technology, the beeping monitors, the IV, the thick straps around Mary Rose's big moon of a belly. If he had had a hat, it'd have been in his hand.

'Knock, knock,' he said. 'I hope these are visiting hours.'

'There are no visiting hours in labor, Ward. I thought you'd done all that reading!' I sounded hysterical, even to my own ears.

'Ward,' said Mary Rose flatly. She turned her head on the pillow to look at him, seemed neither happy nor unhappy to see him. It was almost as if she didn't know him, or as if he was simply another intern passing through.

'Dicky called and told me.'

'Told you what?'

'About being early. About the due date being wrong.'

'Dicky? How did Dicky know?'

At that moment, Betty shuffled in to crank up what in labor-nurse parlance is known as the 'Pit drip.' 'Who's this?' she asked.

'Ward Baron.' He moved to shake her hand, but thought better of it when he saw she was wearing plastic gloves. 'It's my baby.'

'Actually,' said Mary Rose, 'she's not your baby. She's my baby.'

'We're having some problems,' said Ward. 'The mother is angry with me.'

'Well, if she is, I am too,' said Betty. 'Skedaddle! Shoo!' She nudged him out of the way with her hip and checked the fetal monitor. 'No speaka da English? Get lost.'

Mary Rose said nothing but did something oddly conciliatory, considering the circumstances: She extended her hand to Ward. In three big steps he was beside her. Impulsively, he kissed her knuckles.

She said, 'Why does the bride always wear white?'

Ward grinned. He *does* have a grin. Don't ever let anyone tell you that men don't use their looks to their advantage. 'I don't know, Mary Rose, why *does* the bride always wear white?'

'Because people like the dishwasher to match the stove and refrigerator.'

'Groan!'

'You can wait in the waiting room,' said Mary Rose.

The contractions of labor are famous for being indescribable. You can only know them if you've had them, but if you've had them you won't remember them. It's nature's underhanded way of ensuring we're not all only children.

When no one was around, Mary Rose's contractions began. 'Uh-oh, uh-oh,' she said. 'I think that was one. Was that it?'

Betty shuffled in to crank up the drip.

A minute after she left, the contractions escalated.

Mary Rose tried the breathing she'd learned. She stared at the word STRETCH on a box of gloves sitting on the counter, on the sprinkler hanging from the ceiling. She tried to avoid the gold-plated crucifix hanging on the wall beneath the clock. What help could He possibly be? He was the one, after all, who thought live birth was an improvement over an egg in the nest.

'Oh noo noo noo noo noo noo,' whimpered Mary Rose, clutching at the sheet. 'These are really unpleasant, aren't they?'

Betty shuffled in to crank up the drip.

Rex was the anesthesiologist. He was tall and stooped, with a crooked nose that didn't sit square on his face, and long, gentle hands. He walked with tiny stiff steps, obviously in pain.

'Tell me this is not the result of your own handiwork,' said Mary Rose. Between contractions she was more sardonic than usual.

'It's from chopping wood. Not to worry.'

'I've never had one of these,' said Mary Rose. She sat cross-legged on the bed, her pale back bared to Rex. Betty held both of Mary Rose's hands in hers. Rex told Mary Rose to lower her head, some reason having to do with the pressure of the fluid of the spinal cord. Not done properly, an epidural can leave you with a migraine for a week. 'I'm afraid!' squeaked Mary Rose.

'Nothing to be afraid of,' said Rex. 'You've got a perfect back for this. Nothing to it.' He hummed while he worked.

Mary Rose turned to look at him over her bare shoulder. 'That's not "I've Got You Under My Skin" you're singing there, is it?'

He blushed. 'You've got good ears, too, I see.'

Anesthesiology is an art, not a science. Epidurals are meant to anesthetize the fluid around the spinal cord, not the cord, the dura mater, itself. But the needle is inserted by feel. It's a matter of centimeters between an epidural and full spinal block.

During this procedure Rex asked me to leave. Hospital policy. One too many coaches fainting from the sight of a nine-inch needle being threaded between the vertebrae of a loved one.

Next to the nurse's station was the nursery, and it was here, standing outside the window looking in, I ran into Audra Baron. I'm beginning to realize I was born to run into her, and would from time to time, even after the Barons left our city and only returned to visit.

There was a moment when I could have easily passed by, so engrossed was she in watching a big-cheeked Asian newborn, black hair springing straight up from his scalp like wild grass, lying naked beneath a heat lamp. Audra and I watched while a nurse collected his wrinkled feet between her fingers, pressing the bottoms to an ink pad.

'Mary Rose probably won't want visitors after the baby, and certainly none of us, I imagine. Maybe you'd be so kind as to come by the waiting room, just pop you're head in and – '

'Sure,' I said. 'Of course.'

The relief offered by an epidural costs. You trade pain for freedom. Now Mary Rose was bedridden. Without the epidural she could at least struggle to the bathroom by herself, dragging along her IV stand, fetal monitor cords slung around her neck in the manner of rock climbing gear. Now she was stuck.

After a few hours in the same position she said, 'Now I know how veal feels.'

Betty shuffled in to crank up the drip.

Due to the way the needle sat in Mary Rose's back, she could lie only on her right side. The TV was mounted on a ceiling bracket to the left of the bed. There was a full-length mirror in the corner of the room behind the love seat.

'Move that over here,' Mary Rose said.

'You're supposed to watch the birth in this.'

'Isn't there a game on?'

I rolled the mirror over. She had to read the score backward. Mary Rose sighed, her head cradled in the crook of her arm. 'This'll be a piece of cake.'

'I presume you mean the birth and not the game.'

'Of course I mean the birth. You think I'm an idiot?'

The birth, as it turned out, was, relatively speaking, a piece of cake. Still, Mary Rose's labor went on and on.

It was the first game of the first round of the play-offs, and the Blazers gave the entire city hypertension by scraping out a one-point win in overtime. They had been up by as many as twenty-one, then, in the final minutes, the score tied, Ajax Green caught the ball off an inbound pass, tripped over his own feet, and fell out of bounds. The win was due only to a pair of free throws by the Comet.

The next time Betty shuffled in to crank up the drip and check Mary Rose, who was, after nine hours, only five centimeters dilated, she said, 'Can you believe those guys?'

We shook our heads.

At 6:00 I was halfway through a book about mothers and daughters and how to keep your daughter from hating you when she's fifteen. I called Lyle, who had valiantly offered to look after Stella. He had just put her to bed and was washing bottles. He said what men always say to women when faced with reality: 'How do you *do* it?'

At a little after 7:30 P.M., the contractions, previously foothill-shaped on the fetal monitor printout, began looking more like the Rockies.

'I can feel this,' said Mary Rose. 'I'm not supposed to be able to, oh nooo, nooo, nooo!'

'Huh-pah, huh-pah, huh-pah, huh-pah,' I said, leading her in the advanced breathing technique.

'What's wrong? Why do I feel this? I'm not supposed to feel this. I thought that was the whole point of the epidural? What's wrong? Something's gone wrong!' Her voice was small, her big, callused hand damp.

Mary Rose was a Piteous Moaner. I was surprised. I thought she would be a Raging Swearer. All that swagger in everyday life was just that. She was a woman, remember, who had prepared herself to live alone. Not because she necessarily wanted to, but because she knew she would never have how she looked in a miniskirt to fall back on. She was tough, but a Piteous Moaner nevertheless.

The anesthesiologist, whom we'd taken to calling Blushing Rex, hobbled in. 'Hey, hey, hey, take it easy. I was on my way to do another one of these and decided you couldn't wait.' He fiddled with the IV, adjusted the dosage, pulling Mary Rose back from hysteria.

It happened fast. There's just no telling, is there?

Rex left. Betty shuffled in, checked Mary Rose, then left. Dr. Vertamini swept in, leaving the door to the suite open, but pulling a plastic curtain alongside Mary Rose's bed with a snap. Betty unhooked the bottom of Mary Rose's bed and attached, on either side, a pair of black leather troughs, misleadingly called stirrups, for holding Mary Rose's legs.

Suddenly, there she was. Flat on her back, butt in the air, legs spread wide. It was breezy.

Mary Rose said: 'I used to be so modest.'

'Don't start pushing quite yet,' said Betty. She had spit out her gum and was suddenly serious.

She left, the plastic curtain whishing behind her. Dr. Vertamini reappeared and began pulling on scrubs. She tucked her hair into a paper shower cap, peered through a pair of red plastic-rimmed glasses that would have looked at home on the head of a welder. She buffed and peered, peered and buffed. She introduced Mary Rose to the hand grips by the side of the bed.

'Push-push-push-push. C'mon, Mary Rose. Come *on*, Mary Rose. Only you can do this, Mary Rose. Only you can do it.'

Betty rested her hand on Mary Rose's belly, anticipating the next contraction, which she could do more accurately than the fetal monitor.

I stood beside Mary Rose and together we breathed. Inhale, exhale, inhale, PUSH! But the contractions came too fast. The first two breaths became a luxury.

Inhale, then PUSH-PUSH-PUSH-PUSH-PUSH.

Mary Rose squeezed her eyes shut, for fear her eyeballs would fly from their sockets.

Inhale, PUSH-PUSH-PUSH-PUSH-PUSH.

'Do you see anything down there?' she kept asking. 'Do you see anything?'

Betty said, 'A head of dark brown curls, it looks like to me.'

Then another nurse wheeled a plastic crib from the supply closet. A warming device hung above it, not unlike something you'd see at Pizza-by-the-Slice. Mary Rose saw it and sobbed.

'Look, Brooke! It's the thing! It's the thing!'

No one knew what she was talking about. I did. The appearance of the warmer meant Patricia was about to be born.

'C'mon, Mary Rose,' said Dr. Vertamini, 'only you can do this. You're almost there.'

Dr. Vertamini was quick and businesslike. I heard the snip-snip of scissors, heralding an episiotomy, the clip at the top of the perineum that enlarges the vaginal opening just before birth. Then, suddenly, rising up from between Mary Rose's knees, glistening and black-haired, bellowing, one charcoal-gray eye open and squinting up irritably at Mary Rose, there she was.

Patricia Crowder was not what anyone expected. Dr. Vertamini cut the umbilical cord, shiny white and threaded with veins, strong enough to tow a boat, and laid her on Mary Rose's stomach.

There is a type of expensive butter toffee made exclusively in England. It's a rich, milky brown. This was the color of Patricia's skin.

I stared. I knew. There was no Baron in her anywhere.

Mary Rose seemed not at all surprised. She was trembling. She stroked Patricia's slippery brown legs with her fingers.

'Oh, Mary Rose, look how perfect she is. Her hands are just like yours, look.'

No one can resist a miracle.

I was glad Audra was alone in the waiting room. She sat huddled on the edge of her chair, arms folded, legs crossed, watching a Western on TV. She had one of her rich-lady cardigans draped over her shoulders. She stood up when I came in.

I said, 'Everything is fine. Fine. Nine-point-seventy-five pounds, twenty-one and a half inches long.'

'Who does she look like?'

'Well,' I said. 'That's a tough one.'

'Like a little old man, right? Like Otto Preminger?'

'No, no. I would say . . . Well, Audra, I'm just going to say it. I don't think . . . no . . . it's not I don't think. I know. I know for sure. Ward doesn't seem to be the father.'

'What do you mean? How can you tell?'

'She'll be in the nursery soon. See for yourself.'

Audra left the waiting room, her cardigan in a heap, her purse open on a chair.

In the nursery, one nurse fastened an ID bracelet around Patricia's wrist, while another prepared to put in eyedrops.

Audra stared, her trembling hand held over her mouth.

'She's going to be a stupendous beauty. Betty, the labor nurse, already called it. She's been birthing babies for twenty-seven years.'

'She's . . . black,' said Audra. 'Or, wait, we call them something else these days.'

'Well, brown. Technically.'

Patricia, of course, was the daughter of Derik Crawshaw.

'She's as lovely as a newborn can be, isn't she?' Audra

chuckled. She laughed and slapped her thighs. The tears ran down her face.

Stella, I can assure you, is the daughter of Lyle. Just look at her skinny toes.

13

That night when I left the hospital it was drizzling. Who knew how late it was. During daylight saving time, four o'clock and nine o'clock looked the same; the sky a never-changing hue of bunny-rabbit gray. The rhododendrons were all in bloom, hot pinks and purples, as garish as an aunt too old to wear such loud lipstick.

I thought of Mary Rose alone in her hospital room, the nurse bringing Patricia in to her every few hours. Patricia in her pink waffle-weave baby blanket, her tiny pink hat, toffee-colored hair and skin. I wondered if Mary Rose was hungry, ringing that damn button for a nurse to come with something, some saltines, some juice. It's called labor for a reason, but for some reason they always fail to feed you. No bricklayer would ever be accorded such disrespect. Lyle brought me a Big Mac and a vanilla milkshake. Will Mary Rose call Derik? Will he bring her a milkshake? Or no, Derik would be in Utah with the rest of the Blazers. Derik, the father. Impossible to believe.

I could not go home. I could not talk to the back of Lyle's head about this, not just yet. I decided to stop at Donleavy's to pick up some things. Stella's new favorite foods were yams and strawberries. I could get some of those. I could get non-fat milk, and Cocoa Krispies for Lyle.

Donleavy's has the small, narrow shopping carts of yore,

not the wide-bodied models proffered by supermarkets, where a pair of second-graders can sit in the basket quite comfortably, with room to spare for groceries. I went up and down the aisles, feeling like I was playing grocery store, shopping for plastic fruit, clot-red apples, and curvaceous bananas that looked related to the boomerang.

How long had Mary Rose known? She must have known, must have lain awake at night, must have speculated. Then again, in a lot of ways Mary Rose was like a very young girl, or a woman nearing menopause; the fact of pregnancy didn't seem to have much to do with her. She probably put it in the same category as taking a cruise, or hosting a foreign-exchange student. She never dated, and probably presumed love, like purchasing a winning raffle ticket, would happen to someone else. (Love, that is lust, that is the result of lust, which was Patricia.) She probably didn't even keep track of her period. She probably thought, if she thought about it at all, that it was once with Derik, and dozens of times with Ward, so what were the odds?

I felt partially responsible. After telling Lightning Rod McGrew that I had just had a baby, that sitting down was a dicey proposition, much less what he was suggesting, I was too humiliated to go straight back into the bar. I went outside and walked around. Remember, this was the first time I had been out of the house since Stella was born. The world was new. I wandered into a popular boutique that sold adorable merchandise no one needs – ceramic salt and pepper shakers, light-switch plates shellacked with tiny pictures of cowboys and silver stars, candlestick holders, curious implements of massage that looked like three-dimensional renderings of things found in deep space – and spent a good hour happily trying on earrings. When I returned to the hotel bar, Mary Rose and Derik were gone. I assumed they'd gone to hear some jazz, like we'd discussed. Later, when I asked her where they'd disappeared to, she'd said they'd gotten something to eat.

Which was probably also true.

Mary Rose probably never suspected, until, of course, she was given a new due date; then she must have known. Which accounted for her benevolent attitude toward Ward while she was in labor: You want custody of *this* baby? Good luck.

I stopped, there in Donleavy's, inspecting a particularly arthritic-looking yam, realizing how much I loved this kind of thing in a story. The twist that causes you to have to go back and rethink everything that's come before. I loved it like a keepsake, like an ordinary ring worn by someone beloved who'd died. Or like a Christmas carol, not one of the over-played ones. On the heels of this I felt homesick, not for Stella, like I usually did, but a wallop of longing for the inane business of getting a movie together. I'd forgotten about movies, how much I'd once loved them.

On the heels of *this* was the realization that I hadn't thought about Stella in at least a half an hour. I was here having my life, musing about Mary Rose and the size of the modern-day shopping cart, and Stella was home with Lyle, probably playing with her stacking blocks. She was having her life, which was a life apart from me. The idea was devastating. What did this remind me of? It was like getting over losing someone; you missed them every day – every minute as long as an hour – then a day dawned where you only missed them for twenty-three hours and fifty-two minutes, and you rea-lized you were moving on.

This was Stella growing up. First she was a neonate, then she was an infant, now she was a toddler. In a week she would have her first birthday. She was already weaned. Unlike many children who will nurse until it's time to run off to take the SAT, once Stella found solid food she never looked back. This was me getting over the birth of her. This was how it happened. It explained women like Audra, who'd had three sons and could still become obsessed with subtropical gardens and someone else's pregnancy, and now, women like me. You loved your children forever, but you got over the wonder, the marvel, of having had them. Nature only allows you to stagger around lovestruck for so long, your heart so enlarged with love it's on the verge of being a medical condition.

The next morning, when I went to the hospital to pick up Mary Rose, she was sitting on the edge of the high hospital bed in her Jolly Green Giant leggings and XXL black T-shirt, dropping all the tiny and mostly useless samples of soy formula and Pedialyte, something invented to regulate infant electrolytes – whatever those are – doled out by the hospital into a plastic bag.

Patricia was apparently already famous. I was surprised. I heard the nurses talking about her as I passed their station on the way to Mary Rose's room. Word had gotten around that her father was the Comet. As a result, Patricia – suddenly everyone was admiring her long limbs, her big feet and hands – got an extra dose of rocking and cuddling in the nursery. The nurses, all Blazer fans, peered into Patricia's unfocused charcoal-gray eyes to see if the spark of victory glistened there.

Mary Rose wasn't quite sure how they found out.

'I was grilling some nurse about diapering – why does it take the tenacity of a war correspondent to get them to tell you about basic infant care? They should *know* new moms have spent the last nine months worrying about labor and have no clue about burping. I mean, I'm leaving the building with another human being in a matter of *hours*, and you think they'd be interested in my knowing a few basic facts. What was I saying? Oh, and these came. I think the nurse who brought them in had already peeked at the card.' Mary Rose

nodded toward the window ledge, at a crystal vase of pink
tulips nodding on long, pale green stems. 'From Derik.'

'Wow, those are really beautiful.' They were elegant, sent
straight from some upscale nursery. Some thought – not to
mention cash – had gone into their purchase. I'm ashamed to
say it, but at that moment it struck me: The father of Mary
Rose's baby was a millionaire. I was itching to ask what the
card had said. 'How'd he know?'

Mary Rose gave me a look. 'The miracle of the telephone.'

'Mary Rose, I've got to ask . . .'

'No, I thought it was Ward all along. When I found out I
was due so much earlier, I put two and two together. I can
count. I'm not that much of an idiot.' She rolled her eyes but
smiled. Those polished bathroom-tile teeth of hers. 'I guess
whoever is up there in charge of getting souls into bodies will
use whatever means available, huh?'

'Why didn't you tell me?'

She tipped onto her feet, wincing, then fed her feet into her
clogs. 'To be honest? I thought you might be tempted to run
and tell Audra. You know, one thing no one prepared me for is
standing up. I assumed that sitting down wouldn't feel so hot,
but standing up is worse.'

'I never would have said a word,' I said. I was probably lying.

'Yes, you would have. You would have told Lyle, at least.'

'Yeah, and Lyle would have told all the other elves.'

At that moment a nurse came in brandishing a clipboard.
There was paperwork. I put the plastic bag of samples into
Mary Rose's tote. Another nurse brought in Patricia, who was
still asleep, and dropped her into Mary Rose's arms. A peppy
volunteer, who looked like the kind of woman who never
turned down the chance to be in a talent show, appeared at
the door with a wheelchair; the only real help a new mother
gets from the hospital is a lift to the front door.

*   *   *

Stella and I moved in with Mary Rose. Mary Rose didn't know it, of course, and neither did Lyle. I didn't even know it. At first, Stella and I were just going to stay over night, but once installed, there seemed no reason to leave. It was much nicer than living at my own house. I slept on the nubby brown fold-out sofa and Stella slept next to me in her Portacrib. Patricia slept in a white wicker bassinet next to Mary Rose's bed in the next room. During the day we napped, read, cooked, played with Stella, took the girls out for a walk. Patricia slept a lot, as do all newborns, making motherhood, which is reputed to be so hard, seem astonishingly easy. Piece of cake. It is the last time it is a piece of cake. It is the bachelor party of parenting, that first week. When Patricia was awake we undressed her, inspected her folds, her toenails, the way her hips sat in their sockets, as if she was something ordered from a catalog, an expensive, fragile item that we'd only glimpsed in a picture and now needed to examine thoroughly. Then we had to each have a whiff of her neck.

Mary Rose was a much better roommate than Lyle. The only attention she paid her computer was to check her e-mail twice a day. She cleaned out the tub after she used it. We were the new family model. Two mothers and two babies. Or maybe we were the ancient family model. I'm reminded of all those countries, whose names I don't know, but I'm sure they're out there, where the women and the children live together, and the men show up once in a while for their conjugal visits. Men are always whining about being roped into commitments they don't want to make. This could be a happy alternative.

'But in those countries,' said Mary Rose, walking Patricia back and forth across the living room, which was about five giant steps, 'isn't the husband always the same guy?'

'Maybe what I'm talking about is more like a sorority.'

We ate Ben & Jerry's at night – we each had our own private

pint – and watched basketball, our daughters cuddled in our laps. Stella gave no signs of walking yet, which put her behind the developmental curve. Her pediatrician said it was because she began talking early, and rather than walk to get something for herself, she would rather sit and issue orders. 'Like mother, like daughter,' Lyle had remarked. This was the kind of thing I didn't have to put up with at Mary Rose's. That, and Mary Rose managed to be able to put a dirty glass in the dishwasher without having to be asked.

Because it was the play-offs, there was never a night without basketball on TV. The Blazers had advanced to the second round. We hooted like idiots when the camera lingered on Derik sitting on the bench, elbows on his knees, white towel slung around his handsome celebrity neck. Patricia, there's Daddy! With no men around, we wore rag socks under our bathrobes. We clapped with our feet. Stella yowled with delight, then forgot why she was yowling, which she sometimes did, and started to cry.

Once, while Derik was on the line for a free throw, the TV announcer called him 'a fine young player who just became a father.' Mary Rose's hand flew to her mouth. It was as if she had a crush on him, and now the whole school knew! I realized I had to revise my whole thinking about having children. Maybe getting pregnant is a good project for a young couple after all. Mary Rose and Derik weren't dating, but who knew? Maybe becoming parents together was the equivalent of enduring law school or the Peace Corps, or something. Calamity brings people together, after all, and what provided a greater sense of on-going calamity than raising a child?

A week to the day after Mary Rose came home from the hospital, a Saturday, there was a crisis, the likes of which only a woman who has given birth can appreciate. It's the true unspoken challenge of childbirth. Labor and delivery have nothing on this, and yet, it remains cloaked in secrecy. There are no coaches for this. No one has seen fit to market a soothing tape of Amazonian waterfalls and humpback whale song to ease the way. How can I put this? There are no genteel ways. There are coarse ways and there are awkward ways. Mary Rose had not gone to the bathroom since Patricia was born. She had peed, but not the other. It was time for the other. Just when everything was beginning to heal up, tighten up, return to its rightful size and place.

Mary Rose was in the bathroom, bleating. I had just made us some marshmallow Rice Krispie squares. Stella was in the middle of the kitchen floor, playing with the vegetable steamer. I heard Mary Rose crying and knew what was going on. Ouch ouch ouch ouch ouch ouch ouch. When men talk about how passing a kidney stone must be like giving birth, they've got it wrong; passing a kidney stone is more like *this*.

The phone rang, and since I lived there, or felt like I did, I answered.

'Mary Rose?' It was Ward. Ward! Is it possible that after all this I'd sort of forgotten about Ward? After Patricia was born, he'd dropped out of sight. I had expected a scene, thought that once he got a look at the baby who was not his daughter, he would have stormed into Mary Rose's room, demanded to know the meaning of this. That seemed like Baron-ish behavior to me: Life doesn't go according to plan, and so an explanation is required. Someone must be held accountable for such disappointment. Instead, Ward did nothing. Folded up his tent, Bedouin-like, and disappeared into the desert of making a commercial about a new candy that turns the inside of your mouth green. Now he wanted to come over.

'I have some things for the baby. Things I bought. Before.'

I padded to the bathroom. It was two o'clock and I was still in my bathrobe. I had put a special intensive conditioner in my hair, then forgotten to take it out. On the other side of the bathroom door there were the same sorts of sounds you might hear in a movie about demonic possession. Poor Mary Rose! I clenched my teeth, abs, bowels, asshole, and everything else clenchable, in solidarity. 'Who is it?' she moaned.

'Uh, Ward. Ward wants to come over.' Into the receiver I said, 'I don't think it's such a good time.'

'No,' said Mary Rose, 'it's fine. Tell him it's fine.'

'Are you sure?' I said through the door.

'God dammed! God dammed!' she screamed. I have been through this myself. All mothers have. In fact, it is this very thing, and not the specter of going through labor again, that has limited family size. Labor you may forget; this you *never* forget.

'It'll only be for a few minutes,' said Ward. 'Just to drop off a few things.' He sounded piteous. I remembered the day he played with Stella at Starbucks, and all those push-ups he said he did in preparation for the Perry Neal massage. From the bedroom I heard Patricia meowing, awake and needing to be fed. From the living room floor, where Stella was surrounded by books, I heard her say, 'Stellamammobook.' She wanted me to read to her.

'Sure,' I said. 'We're here. Come whenever.'

At that instant, the bathroom door, momentarily stuck in its jamb, flew open, banging against the hallway wall. Mary Rose's hands were still wet from the sink; she wiped them on the leg of her red sweatpants, tugged at her growing-out hair. 'When is he coming? Did he say today?'

'Sometime today.'

'Derik's coming today. I thought today was tomorrow already. He can't come today. Where's the phone?' Mary Rose tried to call Ward everywhere: home, office, pager, car, cell. 'This is all I need,' she cried.

'Look, think of it this way. Who's Ward really? An old boyfriend. A friend, a well-wisher. And who's Derik? Patricia's dad, sure, but also really just a well-wisher. It'll be like a little open house.' I was practicing this voice for when I would get to tell Stella that people are essentially good, and nothing bad will happen to you in life if you have positive thoughts.

Naturally, they arrived within fifteen minutes of each other. It was that hermaphroditic time of day between six and seven, afternoon this time of year, but technically evening, when no one knew what to do with themselves. Too early for dinner, but too late to start thinking about anything beyond ordering out. We had just made some tapioca pudding. Stella had had a bath in the kitchen sink, which had steamed up the windows in the entire apartment, making the whole place smell like lavender.

I heard the downstairs door open, and peeked out the window in the front door, down the stairs, to where Ward was hauling in a long box, one of those boxes about which is always said, 'It's not heavy, just awkward!' He couldn't seem to get the box and his feet inside the entryway at the same time. I knew the box: It contained one of those wind-up swing things that swing so energetically you're convinced your kid is going to be catapulted over the top, which will be her early training for roller-coaster riding.

He pushed the box up the stairs ahead of him. I opened the door, and Ward shoved it in, but the box was too long for the narrow hallway. It ran into the hall closet door, yet still hung out the front door. I was reminded of trying to force a queen-size box spring around corners.

'Here, it's for her,' said Ward. He smelled of the world, of rain, two-day-old cologne and cigar. He needed to shave. 'I didn't know what else to do with it.' He, and the box, took up the entire hallway. It was huge! Ward was huge! His leather jacket, huge! Outside, it was drizzling the usual existential drizzle. Ward stamped his big booted feet on the doormat. The windows rattled in their frames. The tapioca quavered in its bowl. We were all soft and small in here; we never got dressed, read paperback books, slept with stuffed animals, gossiped for hours without regard for topic sentences, drank cocoa in the middle of the day.

Mary Rose pushed herself up from the sofa. Patricia was stowed in the crook of her arm, in a paper diaper and one of the tye-dyed T-shirts purchased for her by Audra, who, like Ward, in a spirit of either genuine largess or perverse upper-middle-class nose-thumbing – you broke our hearts, but we're still *classy* – had also given Mary Rose the things she'd bought for Patricia. It is well known that white babies are as homely as baby birds, with their splotchy skin and broken blood vessels. Patricia, on the other hand, looked like she'd already spent a week on a Caribbean beach, her back and belly as smooth as the caramel wrapped around an apple.

Ward looked, hands in his pockets.

No one can resist a miracle.

Patricia waved her arms at him, as if she were a panicked swimmer, something tiny babies do when they're not wrapped snug in a blanket. They're so used to being folded into a tight spot, that for a week or so after they're born their arms misbehave, like curly hair springing free from a tight hat. 'Do you think she recognizes my voice?' said Ward.

I was moved by his display of vulnerability. I was moved by his bone-headed narcissism and ignorance. Ward, I thought you'd done all that reading! She does not recognize your voice. You have to live with the gestating fetus for that. The truth is, you never read a word, did you? You surfed the Web one night when you were bored. But what business is it of mine? I smiled. He was making an effort, after all.

'I'm sure she does,' said Mary Rose. Mary Rose the Practical, Mary Rose the Levelheaded, was also Mary Rose the Kind.

Then, a knock at the door. A shave-and-a-hair-cut-five-cents! knock. *Dut-dut-dut-dut-dut, dut-dut!* We hadn't heard anyone clopping up the stairs. Whoever was knocking had also tiptoed. I opened it, since I lived there.

Derik 'The Comet' was taller than I remembered. Taller, with a bigger Adam's apple, bigger wrists, bigger big shoes. He said, 'Hey, how you doin'.' Then smiled.

'Derik, come in,' said Mary Rose.

He squeezed in beside Ward and the box with the swingy thing. I don't think he stooped, but I seem to remember him like a nine-foot Christmas tree in an eight-foot room. In the ten months since I'd last seen him in person, he'd filled out in the chest, bought a reasonable gold watch, took one of those classes that they send professional athletes to, classes that teach you how to deal graciously with people who can't help but act demented in your presence. He nodded his head at me, at Ward, then looked at Mary Rose.

Without a word, she stepped forward, placed Patricia in his arms. He looked down, puckered his lips just a little.

Ward, who looked like a foundling next to Derik, cleared his throat, then cleared it again. 'She's going to be a knock-out.'

'She is pretty fine.' Derik looked at Mary Rose. 'Good job, Mary Rose.'

I was expecting Mary Rose to do her hair-tucking thing, to look grateful. Instead, she walked right up to where he rocked their baby, cupped the back of her sweet head with her hand.

Derik turned to Ward and stuck out his hand. *The hand that was responsible for landing the Blazers in the second round of the play-offs!* I worried that I might be panting. 'Derik Crawshaw,' he said. *Duh! Is this what they taught you in celebrity school?*

'Ward Baron,' said Ward.

'He's my cousin,' I said, in an attempt to head off any conversational weirdness at the pass.

'Actually, the guy I used to date,' said Mary Rose. Oh, I knew this impulse. Now that she was a mother, she wanted her life to be free of duplicity, subterfuge, complications inspired by cowardice. A noble impulse that always vanishes when faced with the specter of Santa Claus.

'Just friends, now, though,' said Ward. 'I hope.'

Derik lifted up Patricia closer to his face, which hovered near the ceiling. Do babies get vertigo? 'Where are the diapers? I think we have ourselves a situation.'

Mary Rose lunged toward the diaper bag leaning against the other side of the coffee table, and I lunged toward the bedroom, where I knew there were diapers stacked beneath the changing table. We clunked heads, the Two Stooges. We tripped over stuffed animals, over the Portacrib shoved over in the corner. What was he suggesting? Was he suggesting what we thought he was suggesting? Was the Comet, the best sixth man the Blazers had had in a decade, with his seventy-nine percent field goal average and record as the third best rebounder off the bench in the league, going to change a diaper? TV news, where were you?

'I got three little bros I practically raised. I am the diaper-changing king. I can do it left-handed in the dark. I can do two at once.' Mary Rose escorted him to the changing table.

I realized we could never have our men visit us here for conjugal visits. This was a womb, a nest, a pouch. It wasn't fit for any kind of entertaining, and finally, the reason we want to get out and be with our men is that we want to be entertained, and they are so entertaining. What I'm saying is, I had a sudden, overwhelming urge to debrief with Lyle.

I went and found the phone, which one of us had left under an oven mitt in the kitchen. I called home and left a message that Stella and I were coming home, and that we wanted to be taken out for dinner. Preferably that Tex-Mex place. When I came back in the living room, Ward was holding Stella. She fingered the zippers on his jacket, then put her finger on his lips. 'Duggie doo doo!' she said, and hit her own forehead with the palm of her hand.

'I love a woman who laughs at her own jokes,' said Ward.

Then something bizarre happened. Ward passed Stella back to me, cleared his throat, checked his watch. He really had to be going. There was an edit session, an appointment with the car guy to get his plugs readjusted.

'Tell Mary Rose and, uh, tell them I'll catch up with them another time.'

'It was nice of you to bring this by.'

'What the hell, huh?'

He opened the door, and there, standing on the top step, not four inches from the door, stood Dicky, eavesdropping.

14

We all knew Dicky was odd, but no one thought he was dangerous. This sentiment gets my vote for Top Cliché of the Modern World, what everyone always says when something like this happens. It's because no one can bear knowing that someone is dangerous, but there's nothing to be done about it. Life is simply dangerous, and there's no one you can call and report it to.

The half dozen times in my life I've been the recipient of a middle of the night phone call, it has always been a breather, or a brat asking if my refrigerator was running (go catch it!). Now, however, there is too much television news. Also, I'm a mother. So even though I've never answered to anyone but the brat, I always expect The Worst, even though Stella sleeps in the next room, not seven steps away from me, our tiny house double-key dead-bolted and patrolled by the geriatric Itchy Sister, who spends her nights pacing, when she's not scratching and biting her butt.

When the phone rang at 3:37 A.M. – what did we do before the digital clock? – I grabbed it on the first ring, afraid it would wake up Stella, who had slept through the night for nine nights running, a record. It was about three weeks after Patricia was born.

The voice on the other end was soft, flattened by shock. Mary Rose.

'Oh, God, is it Patricia?'

'Who is it?' Lyle muttered, curling into my back.

'I'm okay. I'm at the hospital,' she said. 'They want somebody to drive us home.'

'What's going on? What's happening? Did she stop breathing?'

'Oh, God, no, nothing as horrible as that. It's Dicky. He tried to take Patricia.'

'I'm coming right now.'

The odd thing about Lyle is that despite his fastidiousness, he does like a good emergency. It is the drama, of course. It was the drama of our speedy courtship and frantic lovemaking in hotel beds previously slept in by the top players of the NBA that led to the altar and, eventually, to Stella. This may be what accounts for his dedication to Realm of the Elf, where everyday he gets a chance to chop up an ogre, and, on a good day, avoid bleeding to death.

When I told him what happened, and that I needed to go to the hospital, he bounded from bed, pulled on a pair of hiking shorts, threw on the kitchen lights and started making coffee. He reassured Itchy Sister, blinking nervously from the depths of her plaid dog bed. He said he would watch Stella as long as I needed and wait by the phone in case there was anything he could do. If need be, he would call in sick to work. (Like many people, for Lyle this was not an unpleasant prospect. Having a chance to miss a day or two of a job you despise for a genuine calamity makes the calamity itself feel like a holiday.)

'Don't forget your jacket. Think you should grab one for Mary Rose? And some change for the pay phone.'

The hospital closest to the triplex was affiliated with the Episcopal church, and was thus in every way like a five-star hotel. It sprawled over several blocks, connected by a sky bridge of smoky glass.

When I arrived Mary Rose was in the waiting area, flipping uncomprehendingly through the recent issue of *Travel & Leisure*. A movie played on the big-screen TV. Patricia slept beside her in her car seat, making little sucking noises.

Mary Rose was wearing her red sweatpants, a T-shirt advertising an apple-tasting festival at a local nursery, and a pair of old, laceless pink high-tops. Her right hand was wrapped in gauze, which made it difficult for her to sign her release forms. A police officer, a black woman with long red nails, a daisy painted on the end of each one, and a waist so tiny her holster wrapped around her almost twice, said they would be in touch.

I brought the car around and asked about the hand.

'Powder burn.' She waved it off. 'Patricia almost slept through the entire thing, thank God. Even under the best of circumstances I look at her and think, "Mary Rose, you have created a hostage to fortune. Shame on you."' Her eyes leaked tears.

Mary Rose is a terrible reporter. It's one of the things I admire most about her; she somehow escaped the feminine need to explain, expound, tease out, overanalyze. I am an archivist, a collector of data. I feel guilty if someone asks the time and I don't have it.

As I understand it, what happened was this: Mary Rose had gone out to the grocery store at around 10:30 for some diapers. It was the usual new-mother thing; she had gone to the store earlier in the day for the express purpose of getting diapers, then had forgotten to buy them. She put the only one she had left on Patricia at about 8:30, and knew it wouldn't last until morning. She bundled Patricia up, put her in her car seat, put the car seat in the car, drove to the store. There was no more popping out to the store for her. She was exhausted.

Driving home, Patricia fell asleep. When Mary Rose got in the apartment, she thought, 'Patricia will be up in a few hours anyway, I'll just wait until she wakes up,' then kicked off her shoes and fell on her bed.

Minutes later (it turned out to be a little over an hour), she woke up. She thought she'd heard Patricia stirring, but Patricia was still asleep, her little body bent over forward in the seat, folded over like a sleeve. Mary Rose worried she couldn't breath in this position, propped her back up, and went to the bathroom. She was still struggling on that front. She sat on the plastic blow-up doughnut they gave her at the hospital, and read an article in a horticulture magazine on the return of the pansy. Mary Rose was intrigued; she was unaware the pansy had gone anywhere.

She didn't know how long she was in there. She came out, walked through the living room, where the lights were off. The only light on in the apartment was the one on her beside table, and she saw through the doorway that Patricia and her car seat were not where she'd left them, and as she ran to the bedroom, she passed someone there in the dark, in the hallway by the front door. It was Dicky, standing in the dark, one hand on the doorknob, the other gripping the handle of Patricia's car seat. What was this? This was not right. Was this some arrangement she had made but forgotten about? Had she asked him to baby-sit at midnight, then lost track of the time? It couldn't be what it looked like, Dicky Baron walking out the door in the middle of the night with her baby.

'Mary Rose!' He practically shouted. She'd obviously surprised him. 'I was going to leave a note. Actually, I was going to call. Calling was a better plan. I'm taking this baby to my brother. You broke my brother's heart. He wants this baby more than you do, so I'm taking her. To my brother.' Later, Mary Rose would tell the investigating officer that it sounded as if he was delivering a speech.

Mary Rose the Levelheaded, Mary Rose the Practical. Mary Rose had, as you know, prepared herself to spend her life alone. Tacked to the back of her orange-crate bed stand was a hammock that looked not unlike Stella's waterproof nylon bath toy bag attached by suction cups to the wall over our tub. In the hammock was the .25 ACP, the type of small-caliber automatic about which gun lovers say, 'It's the perfect weapon if you don't want to hurt anyone.' It had been given to Mary Rose by her father, the best he could do after her mother died, to help prepare her for life.

But now Mary Rose was the mother, something Dicky hadn't counted on. To Dicky, mothers were forgetful, fat, and milky. They were that, but they were also something else. Dicky was surprised Mary Rose had said nothing. That's the other thing mothers are: chatterboxes. They give birth, then never shut up. But she had nothing to say to him. She took three longs steps into her room, reached behind her nightstand, and pulled out the gun. She pointed it at his nose.

'Put her down, Dicky.'

'Whoa! Look, listen to me here. Listen to what I have to say before, before you go all postal on me. Just listen.'

'Put her down or I will shoot you. I will kill you and I won't care, and no one will blame me. Put her down now.' She didn't think she would do it. Not really. Shooting the place up was something a guy would do. She thought the gun was sort of more of a bargaining chip than a weapon of destruction, a conversational gambit.

'Jesus, Mary Rose. Relax a little here. Look, I'm going to level with you. All right? I need a break here. I need to get something going. Let me just take her downstairs for the night. You can call the cops now. Actually, count to ten, let me get downstairs first. They'll swarm around for a day or two – '

'Put her down –' said Mary Rose. What was with the outfit? It was the middle of June and Dicky was all bundled up. A black Blazers cap on backward, one of those billowy oiled dusters that looked as if they'd keep you dry in a typhoon, and a brand-new pair of L.L. Bean boots. Do you know those boots? With the rubber sole and leather upper? Mary Rose knew those boots. She had a pair. They were boots for slogging around the mud in the rain, when you expected to be outside for a while. If he was just taking Patricia downstairs, what was he doing in these clothes?

'I know I just said a night, but really I'll need two or three days. No one would buy it if it was just a night. Kidnapping a big basketball star's baby. That's what I'm going for. Do you see the appeal? He's a millionaire, but nothing can replace his little girl. You're one of those bossy women who waited too long to have kids, but now you've got her and you're dying with love? Just think about what a positive statement this will make to the world. All about the power of love. It'll be like that Mel Gibson movie, *Ransom*. In fact, here's an idea, here's something I'll offer you – you can find her! How would that be? Then you'll have a story, too. You'll be a hero, too. I won't hurt her, Mary Rose. In fact, just tell me what she eats, and I'll make sure she gets some food.'

Mary Rose knew what those shoes were for. They were shoes you wore when you were going to dig a hole. It was May, but the ground was still boggy. Later, in court, Dicky would claim he never had any intention of hurting Patricia, not burying her or anything else. When asked by the prosecutor what he was doing with a brand-new shovel in the trunk of his car, he would say that, inspired by Mary Rose, he'd decided to take up gardening.

It's unclear what happened next. Mary Rose said he turned his back on her. He said, 'Suit yourself,' turned, and opened the door. He opened the door, and Mary Rose opened fire. A mom's got to do what a mom's got to do. Patricia, in her car seat bumped all the way down the stairs, landing unhurt in the entryway. She was, by that time, screaming.

*   *   *

Mary Rose and I returned to my house to find Lyle making breakfast, billowing cheese omelets, toast dotted with islands of thick butter, and unnaturally bright orange juice made from concentrate. As you know, my love for him is a faulty plug that shorts out now and then, but this was one of his most endearing moments: mistaking harrowing urban experience for something rural and taxing, as if Mary Rose and I had just come in from pounding in fence posts or rounding up cattle. Stella, mercifully, was still asleep.

Mary Rose took one bite of omelet, pressed her napkin to her eyes, and started to cry. 'I'm all right,' she said. 'I'm all right.'

'And Patricia's all right?' said Lyle.

'They want, they want me to have her hearing checked in a while. Guns are loud inside. They're never that loud in the movies. It takes only one loud blast to . . . anyway, they said I should keep on it. Her hearing.' Mary Rose tucked her hair behind her ears, over and over.

'What was that joke you told me once?' said Mary Rose.

'I hope I've told you more than one joke since we've known each other,' I said.

'You know . . .' She blew her nose. 'It was more of an anecdote. About that movie you wanted to work on, then it turned out to be a nightmare? The punchline was "Who do I have to sleep with to get *off* this picture?" That's how I feel.'

'Well, it's over now.'

Then I heard a thump-thump-thump from Stella's room. She was kicking the rungs of her crib, my wake-up call. I picked her up and settled her on my hip. We made our morning tour of her room, stopping to count the puppies on her *101 Dalmatians* poster, look in the mirror, point at the clock. We waved hello to Dad at the kitchen sink, then moved to the high chair, where she ate rice cereal and applesauce, then back to her room, where I changed her diaper, stopping momentarily to admire the bits of peas in a project the consistency of pâté, dabbing some Desitin in all the tender cracks and folds, then wrestling her into a romper, before giving her an eyedropperful of vitamins/fluoride and brushing her hair.

The most interesting, and not incidentally cruelest, fact is that life goes on. I once heard someone say one of the evils of television was that by juxtaposing a report of a plane crash with a mouthwash commercial it trivialized our tragedies. True, but guess what? After the funeral you still need to floss.

In the afternoon, after Mary Rose had slept, she wanted to go back to the triplex. She wanted to have a shower and get dressed and deal with the mess. The police, who in our city are notorious for arriving late at the scene, then plugging the victim, wanted to 'assess the situation' before Mary Rose got out her bucket and Pine-Sol, assuming that was what one used.

The media has been singularly unhelpful in that area: who cleans up the blood and how? I brought along a book my mother sent me when Lyle and I got married: *Mary Ellen's Helpful Hints: Fast-Easy-Fun Ways of Solving Household Problems*. Lyle and Stella went off to the Indoor Family Play Gym. I told Lyle if I heard that he had been ogled by any of the mothers there, I would string him up by his balls. He swatted me on the arm as he left to show his appreciation for my concern.

Officers Splevak and Evans were sitting in their car in the driveway when we arrived. They were courteous and rather bored. The guy who came to my house and sprayed for carpenter ants was livelier than these two.

Officer Splevak, whose poly-blend slacks pulled at the back of his pumped-up thighs, asked Mary Rose to re-enact what happened. Mary Rose showed how she reached for her weapon behind the orange-crate nightstand, then held the gun on Dicky until he turned his back on her and started to leave.

'Did he really think this would work?' Mary Rose asked again and again. 'How could he think this would work?'

The officers pretended not to hear her, which I thought was verging on inhumane. They muttered between themselves. Officer Evans was a woman, and therefore the scribe. She dutifully wrote down Mary Rose's version of events, then scraped some of the blood from the floorboard. There was very little. I was surprised. Mary Rose was grateful. Somehow the fact of there being relatively little to clean up meant that she would not have to move.

Officer Evans saw me take *Mary Ellen's Helpful Hints* from my bag and said, 'White vinegar should do the trick.'

It did.

I pleaded with Mary Rose to stay with us for a few nights, but she refused. When I drove off she was standing on her deck, one foot up on her wooden planter boxes, beautiful Patricia plunked on her hip, looking like a pioneer.

I arrived home from Mary Rose's apartment to find a message from Dicky on my answering machine. He was in the hospital and he wanted to see me.

He was alone in his room, chuckling at something on MTV. He, or someone, had combed his thinning blond hair. An IV drip was taped to the back of his fat hand.

Dicky never really looked much like Nick Nolte, despite the now ancient rantings of the Associated Press. He was square and blond with light close-set eyes, but there was never anything about him that suggested he could battle evil or win anyone's heart. Still, against the toothpaste-colored sheets of his hospital bed, Dicky looked tanned and . . . the word I keep wanting to write is content. It was eerie. He was animated in the way people are when they've survived a great disaster.

Dicky's wound was not, apparently, very serious. Or rather, it was serious, but in an unusual way. Mary Rose shot him in the upper portion of his butt. The bullet had missed all his major organs, and, due to either the small caliber of the bullet, or the dampness of the powder, had not quite reached his spine, but rather sat, according to the X-rays, within centimeters of it, pressing on the subdura mater that surrounds the dura, the tough but precious stuff that makes up the spinal cord and brain. Removing the bullet was out of the question. The most experienced neurosurgeon wielding the finest instruments might incur permanent damage working that close to the spine.

I stood as far away from his as I could and still be in the room. 'What is this all about?'

'This is even better than I ever imagined. Don't you think? I wasn't going to hurt it anyway. What's its name? The baby? Then, BOOM, she blows me away.'

It didn't seem appropriate to point out that had he been truly blown away, he would hardly be lying there channel-surfing. I said nothing.

'I was doing it for my brother. Just because Ward isn't the real father doesn't mean he isn't the true father. He wanted it more than Mary Rose did. I know. I lived downstairs from her. All she did was hold her back and complain, complain, complain. I was being heroic.'

'She said you were going for the kidnapping-the-famous-athlete's-child angle.'

'That was another idea I had. Right there, working in the moment. Isn't it a gas working in a creative medium? I just thought of it, just like that, when I saw she was going to plug me. But now that I have been shot, do you think there's anything in this? That we could sell. Story rights. It seems like a good hook. It could be a part of *As I Lay Down the Dagger*. Here I am, trying to live a quiet life, a post-fame life, minding my own business, but my brother, who's always wanted a kid is denied at the last minute. Denied, humiliated. And I think, *This isn't right.* The real mother doesn't want the kid, the real father really doesn't want the kid, and here's my brother, hurting. It's kind of wild, huh? Kind of Dostoyevskian, huh? And brother movies are very big this year.'

I looked at him and said nothing. I don't think I'd ever seen him this happy, his big cheeks hiked up around his little eyes in a delirious grin. My feet trembled. My ears were cold. Toxic digestive acids powerful enough to eat through an I-beam sloshed around my stomach.

Presently, Audra and Big Hank walked in. Only weeks before they looked like advertisements for early retirement or iron-fortified vitamins. Now Big Hank looked desiccated and bent, rather than trim and toned. Audra's face was rice-cereal pale, her auburn hair rudely bright.

'I'm glad to see you're feeling well enough to talk to reporters,' said Audra, her voice the quaking whisper of the truly seething.

I glanced at the paper she laid on Dicky's knees. Our city's major newspaper likes to liven up its front page with stories of its citizens. It dutifully covers skirmishes and economic summits above the fold. Below the fold is traditionally reserved for preteen entrepreneurs who earn money for college selling silk-screened T-shirts or, in this case, the misguided behavior of our city's first families.

I scanned the story. There was no comment from Derik, who was in San Antonio.

'Words fail me,' said Audra.

Dicky nodded his head. 'Okay, we can work with that. Brooke, are you writing this down?'

Audra rolled her eyes heavenward. Tears tipped out of her

eyes and onto her cheeks. She whispered: 'I can't believe you came out of me.'

'Aw, Ma,' said Dicky. 'You're so dramatic.'

An intern appeared at the door. He grinned beneath a ginger-orange moustache. He obviously knew this was not just another body in a bed.

Before asking us to excuse him, the intern checked the time, drawing from his pocket a large tarnished silver watch. Big Hank, who had been standing beside Dicky's bed, as inert and pained as a schoolboy in church, perked right up.

'Say, is that an old Elgin you've got there?'

Audra could not contain herself. Decorum may have prevented her thwacking her injured son up the side of his head, but this was too much.

'Hank, goddammit. This is your son here.'

Hank looked up from the watch cradled between his thumbs. His perturbed expression beneath his blond brows said, 'Oh?'

15

We have an alcove off our kitchen that I had used as an office while I was pregnant with Stella. One day, several weeks after the business with Dicky, I came home from Donleavy's to find Lyle in the alcove, blowing dust from the keyboard of the computer. The monitor sat on the small table. He plugged it in.

'Uh-oh, what's wrong with the basement?' I set the groceries on the counter. I had visions of flooding, infestation, one too many dog farts.

A white plastic bag sat on the chair. From it he pulled a mouse pad.

'Witty pop cultural reference.' He displayed the pad as if he was standing before a large audience eager to see: on it was a picture of Micky Mouse. He passed it to Stella, who was sitting on the kitchen floor amid her favorite pots and pans. She stared at the mouse pad, waved it in the air like she was waving at Daddy.

'Come watch while we unlock the wonder pony and hitch a ride on the magical carousel.' He scooped up Stella and propped her on his thigh in front of the monitor. She did not want to let go of the mouse pad. He booted up, and the computer went through its bumps and grinds.

'What about Realm of the Elf?' I said.

He snorted. 'Do you know what they're doing now? In the Realm? They've added some features. Now you can buy a house and get married.'

'I thought elves lived in old tree stumps or something.'

'Yeah, well they did. None of my buddies want to go out and fight monsters anymore. They all meet in the town square and talk about their crummy water pressure. I can do that in real life. In fact, I can do better in real life. We have inch-and-a-half pipes in this house.'

Goofy music filled the kitchen. A character named Reader Rabbit and his buddy Mat the Mouse appeared with a cartoon pop and yattered on about guiding us to the musical meadow. Stella pointed and said something that sounded like *ebullient*. She bounced herself up and down on Lyle's leg. He put her hand on the mouse and clicked it. She laughed, wanted to click it again.

'I have to say, this is a lot more fun now that she's a little older.'

'I've heard about this. The second a kid gets out of diapers the Dad suddenly realizes there was actually a human being sitting in all that shit.'

Lyle gave me a hurt look.

'Sorry,' I said, 'that was a little . . . emphatic. So, anyway, what will you do with yourself? I mean, I presume what you're telling me is that you're giving up on your elf.'

'I thought I'd do some painting.'

'Pictures?'

'No, the bathroom. For starters.'

I put my hands on my thighs and stood up. It was the first time in two years that I was wearing zip-up pants. A pair of inky blue jeans made of stiff, high-quality denim. Elastic waistbands are for the very young, the very sick, and the permanently postpartum. I wasn't quite ready to go back to work yet, but I was ready to get out my bathrobe, metaphorically speaking.

I said, 'I think it's time I started making some phone calls.'

He said, 'Hollywood-type phone calls?'

I said, 'Something. Maybe someone's got something in production up here and needs a line producer.'

He said, 'Anything I can do to help?'

I said, 'Dump Lil Plum. Now.'

'Ha. Lil Plum turned out to be a fifty-two-year-old guard at a state correctional facility – it gets better – on permanent disability with a crippling case of gout.'

'Ooh, baby. Hold me back.'

I made a list of old film contacts. I called Melissa Lee Rottock, my agent, and the executive who had been in charge of producing *Romeo's Dagger* (she had left the film industry and was now selling real estate). I called the local film commission to see what was shooting in town.

That night, the three of us – four of us, including Itchy Sister, who hogs the sofa – sat down and watched the Blazers play their last game of the season. Lyle made some of his killer chicken salad, with lots of pepper and dill. We fed some to Stella, her first chicken salad, and she made that face that makes us want to lie down and laugh till we suffocate. Despite the dazzling play by the Comet twenty-one field goals, eleven rebounds), the Blazers did not advance to the final round of the play-offs, leaving us, and our city, feeling jilted once again.

Six months later we ran into Audra Baron in Puerto Vallarta. It was January, her annual month of madness, and Lyle, Stella, and I were there on one of those three-night/four-day package tours, before I began preproduction on a movie-of-the-week about mermaids. The tour was booked solid with people who wore name tags and never ate anywhere but the hotel for fear a friendly Mexican waiter would press a salad upon them. Their eventual sunburns forced them to lie in the shade of the hotel *palapas*, their arms and legs paved with white wash-cloths taken from their rooms. We didn't care; our fellow tourists were uncomplaining and thought Stella was the most precocious, winsome baby they'd ever seen.

Arne was the recreation director of the hotel, arranging scuba tours and horseback-riding expeditions to hidden waterfalls. He sold his packages mostly around the pool and at the swim-up bar. For his opening gambit he sidestroked up and named the perfume you were wearing. Quite a feat, considering the amount of chlorine in the pool.

He introduced himself as Arne from America, though there was the sound of northern Europe in his voice. He was German but had grown up in Chicago. Burly and brown as a nut, he reminded me of someone. He wore his striped Speedo bikini without a trace of self-consciousness, had gold-rimmed teeth and a huge laugh, a huge scar running down his side that spoke of shark attacks and adventure. He sold Lyle and me an all-day snorkeling package off a beach accessible only by boat, nanny for Stella included.

There is a strip of sidewalk called the *malecon* that runs along Puerto Vallarta's main beach, the natural destination of tourists and locals alike. Here, you could watch the food chain in action; pelicans diving for fish and Mexican teenage boys flirting expertly with their breathtaking girlfriends. Also in evidence was the slightly older version of the couple, sitting on the wrought-iron benches overlooking the sea, she pregnant, with a toddler in a frilly pink dress scampering about, he no-where to be seen.

At the end of the *malecon* there was a spray-paint artist who regularly drew a crowd. He painted singularly hideous sea-scapes and other-worldly sunsets, inspired by third-rate heavy-metal album covers. The templates for his futuristic planets were old jar lids and cheap plates. To dry the paintings he would spray a stream of paint parallel to the surface of the paper, then ignite it. Tricky business; also quite a show. He wore a bandanna over his nose and mouth and listened to ancient cassette tapes of Pink Floyd.

People from my tour, sharp enough to know that serapes and piñatas were not the real Mexico, thought this was it, and bought the paintings to go in the den, on the wall over their pull-out sleepers.

It was here, the last night of our vacation, I saw a woman who looked like Audra, with Arne, his jungle vine of an arm wrapped around her, his brown hand attached beneath her breast, just so. I was not a new mother anymore. Far from it; Stella was walking, played peek-a-boo, sang to the dog. My wits were sharp. There was no mistaking my aunt, with her auburn hair and full cheeks, her nose splashed with freckles. I could tell from the way she leaned into Arne that this was no winter fling. They stood among the circle of onlookers, their faces illuminated by the sudden zot of blue fire. She wore a loose dusty-pink linen shirt tied at the waist, walking shorts, sandals.

I pulled on Lyle's sleeve. 'Look, over there, who's that?'

Lyle was always quick; he was almost as good as a woman that way. He knew what I meant, knew I didn't mean look there's Audra. 'Oh, jeez,' he said, 'it's Dicky Baron.' For that was exactly who Arne looked like.

I walked Stella over to where Audra and Arne stood at the back of the crowd. She walked holding on to my fingers; I knew she was able to go it alone, but couldn't bear to let that happen just yet.

'Well, aren't you a magnificent little thing,' said Audra, extricating herself from Arne. He turned to a couple on the other side of them. The conversation appeared to be about bullfights. Of course Audra didn't see me yet. She was admiring Stella's blue-flowered sundress. No one ever sees the mother of a beautiful child.

207

'Hi, Audra,' I said.

She looked not at all surprised to see me. 'I told you this was a fantastic place, didn't I?' We made the obligatory reference to the rain back home.

'How's Dicky?' I finally asked. I had to know. After Dicky had been released from the hospital last June, he'd moved back home, presumably to be taken care of by Audra.

For a time, he'd entertained a few TV movie offers, much to Audra's displeasure. Eventually, though, TV passed. The injury he sustained from the gunshot wound wasn't great enough to warrant any real interest. Which doesn't mean it wasn't great enough to cause him real suffering.

He was tried and convicted of attempted kidnapping. But since the jails of our city are horrendously over-crowded and Patricia sustained not a scratch, Dicky was given no jail time, and eighteen months probation. Judge Gardstein, who regularly golfed with and often beat Big Hank, claimed it was enough that he was going to spend the rest of his life paying for his 'judgment error' as a semi-invalid.

'Dicky is fine,' said Audra. 'In that Dicky could ever be fine. He sees a lot of doctors these days. They think now that the bullet may cause problems. They're saying it's not as firmly lodged as they thought. Someday it may just decide to pick up and enter his circulatory or lymphatic system. Of course, they can't remove it, either.'

'But he'll be all right? Besides the never-knowing aspect of it?' I didn't really care if he was going to be all right or not, but Audra was his mother.

'It's the story of my life. You'll think I'm superficial – you probably do anyway – but I keep thinking, this is the same problem we have with the house. The keys on the piano are going, but we can't replace them with ivory because, well, you know the story with ivory. And if we switch to plastic we ruin, in Big Hank's words, 'the integrity of the instrument.' So, we just sit there, waiting for the everything to collapse around our ears.' She sighed. 'I got a letter from Mary Rose awhile back.'

'She told me she was going to write.'

'Telling me she wasn't sorry for what she'd done. At first I thought it was sort of, I don't know, pitiless. She wondered if I understood she had no choice. Patricia was *her* child. But, you know, Dicky is *my* child. Even now. She did apologize for calling me an interfering you-know-what. She wrote it on Mowers and Rakers letterhead, the ninny. It should have come on some nice creamy bond.'

'That's generous of you, Audra. After all that's happened.'

'Well. You'll see. Stella's still a tiny thing. It's different when they're all grown up and start ruining their own lives. You're heartbroken, don't get me wrong, but helpless. Heartbroken and helpless as the day they're born.' She sighed, dabbed at her eyes.

We made some talk about getting together once we got home, but we haven't so far. Audra said something funny as Lyle, Stella, and I headed back to the hotel, Stella, now asleep and snoring on Lyle's shoulder. 'Call me if you're ever in the motherhood.'

Sometimes when I find myself driving up the narrow, shady streets of the West Hills, I see the Mowers and Rakers truck parked in front of someone's house, and there is Mary Rose, Patricia a papoose upon her back, standing on a ladder wielding her pruners, or loping across a lawn with a bucket of compost, on her way to some far-flung vegetable garden. She has the energy of ten men, and always had. It helps, of course, that Patricia began sleeping through the night at five weeks.

209

Ours is the friendship of young mothers, which resembles the rhythm of a fire fighter on the job: weeks go by and we don't talk, then, suddenly, a flurry of mad phone calling when one of us finds we have a few hours free. We still have our basketball dates, but not as often. We also have the knowledge that if the other one doesn't phone right back, or has to cancel a coffee date once too often, that it's not personal, simply motherhood. We also have e-mail.

Mrs. Marsh rehired Mary Rose, as has Mrs. Ostly, and almost all the other West Hills neighbors of the Barons who'd let her go when they imagined she was too pregnant and too unmarried to be their gardener. Having the mother of a professional basketball player's child working zoo doo into their perennial beds carried with it a certain cachet. They also enjoyed being viewed as open-minded and nondiscriminatory by employing the single mother of a mixed-raced baby born out of wedlock.

Derik sees Patricia on the weekends when he's in town, just as if he's a normal noncustodial dad. Sometimes he accompanies Mary Rose on her rounds. He stands on some lawn, gently drapes the dozing Patricia over his long forearm, rocks her and rubs her back while patiently answering questions posed by this Lady of the House, or that Captain of Finance and Industry, lured from their homes to ask what it was really like playing with Ajax Green.

Last month his contract was renewed for some obscene amount. He'll start next season. I think he just turned twenty-six. *Sports Illustrated* had a brief article on up-and-comers and named Derik as someone who was maturing nicely, 'quite possibly because of the birth of his first child.' So cozy and misleading, isn't it? A harmless little remark like that in a magazine. It makes all the harmless little remarks in all magazines seem suspect, doesn't it?

Since Patricia and Stella's birthdays are only two weeks

apart, Mary Rose and I held a joint birthday party in our backyard. We invited a few children from the Indoor Play Gym, the Assistant D.A. down the block and her son, who was now almost three, the cellist Mary Rose had met in prenatal water aerobics. She'd had a daughter, too. Miraculously, the sun shone, the lilacs were in bloom, and none of the children were contagious for strep throat, which was going around.

I also bought them a thirty-seven-dollar chocolate cake. Stella ate the purple flowers from around the edge one by one – she's as meticulous as her father – then suffered a terrific case of diaper rash the next day. We got some nice pictures, however. Of the birthday, not the diaper rash.

While Mary Rose and I were in the kitchen making fresh coffee for the moms and filling bottles with juice for the babies, she confessed that she'd started seeing Rex. Remember Blushing Rex, Anesthesiologist? He turned out to be an outdoorsman, also newly divorced.

'Mary Rose, Mary Rose. That is fantastic. Divorced guys are great because they've experienced the miracle of cause and effect.'

She raised an eyebrow, said nothing.

I told Mary Rose it would be good for Patricia to have as many adult males in her life as possible. I said it takes at least four adults to raise one baby, and wouldn't I know?

Mary Rose said there was Derik.

I said, no, *really* in her life: refusing to change her diaper, holding her only when she's happy. Remembering how much I championed poor Ward, Mary Rose didn't think much of my ideas.

Anyway, I believe a girl should have a father so, if nothing else, she can see what men are like, up close. I told Mary Rose that Patricia would come to idolize Derik because he was never around. Mary Rose shrugged her wide shoulders and lit a cigarette, blew the smoke out of the side of her mouth.

'And what about you, what's new with you?' She narrowed her brown eyes, looked at me very closely. 'I think you're pregnant. I'm a mother. I can tell these things.'

A NOTE ON THE AUTHOR

Karen Karbo is the author of two previous novels, *The Diamond Lane* and *Trespassers Welcome Here*, each of which was named a *New York Times* Notable Book of the Year. Her nonfiction has appeared in *Vogue*, *Esquire*, *Entertainment Weekly*, *The New Republic*, and *The New York Times*. She is currently a contributing editor to *Condé Nast Sports for Women*. She grew up in Southern California and now lives in Portland, Oregon with her husband, daughter and stepchildren.

A NOTE ON THE TYPE

The text of this book is set in Berling roman. A modern face
designed by K. E. Forsberg between 1951–58. In spite of its youth
it does carry the characteristics of an old face. The serifs
are inclined and blunt, and the g has a straight ear.